FLORA MACDO

was born in 1872, a twin daughter
Classics at King's College, Univers
an Anglican clergyman. Her mother was a niece of George Grote,
the historian of Greece and co-founder of the University of London.
In 1892, when university education was still unusual for a woman,
she went to Newnham College, Cambridge, where she read History.
For a short time she was an actress but the ill-health which dogged
her life—recurrent attacks of bronchial asthma—and the tragic
death of her fiancé from typhoid fever in India in 1904 drew her
back into her family circle, where she quietly passed the rest of her
life.

In 1901, under the pseudonym of Mary Strafford, she published
her first book *Mrs. Hammond's Children*, a collection of stories for
children. *The Third Miss Symons*, her first novel, was published in
1913, was highly praised but soon was forgotten with the coming
of the First World War. Her second novel, *The Rector's Daughter*
was published eleven years later, in 1924, and it is these two novels
which best express her artistic genius. Another novel, *The Squire's
Daughter* followed in 1929 and a collection of short stories, *The
Room Opposite* was published posthumously in 1935. F. M. Mayor
died in 1932.

The Third Miss Symons

by F. M. Mayor. With a Preface by John Masefield

New Introduction by Susan Hill

Virago
London

Published by VIRAGO Limited 1980
5 Wardour Street, London W1V 3HE

First published 1913

Copyright © F. M. Mayor 1913
Copyright © The Estate of F. M. Mayor 1932

Introduction Copyright © Susan Hill 1980

ISBN 0 86068 131 9

Printed in Great Britain by The Anchor Press Ltd
and bound by Wm Brendon & Son Ltd
both of Tiptree, Essex

NEW INTRODUCTION

IT WOULD be wrong to describe Flora Macdonald Mayor as a forgotten novelist, and inaccurate, too, at least to a certain extent, to claim that she is underrated. Her work is certainly far too little known in relation to the greatness of her talent. But her masterpiece, *The Rector's Daughter* (1924), is in print again (Penguin Modern Classics) and the ranks of its admirers are steadily increasing. Those who do discover her, pass the word along: biographical and critical studies of her are under way both here and in the United States, and this republication of *The Third Miss Symons* has been long awaited and can only help to increase her present-day reputation.

There is not, alas, much more of her fiction to be read, and what there is scarcely deserves resurrection. Her first novel, *Mrs. Hammond's Children* (published under the pseudonym of Mary Strafford), is really interesting only by contrast with what came later. *The Squire's Daughter* (1929) is so poor that I find it hard to believe it was written by F. M. Mayor at all; a collection of mystery tales, in the sub-M. R. James tradition, *The Room Opposite* (published posthumously in 1935), are entertaining and certainly hold their own as minor representatives of a rather creaking genre.

But it is on the two novels alone that her claim to an important place in twentieth-century English fiction rests. They are works of a quite remarkable psychological depth, subtlety and assurance: they reveal a creative imagination and perceptiveness of devastating clarity and honesty, and demonstrate a technical mastery of the novel form which seems to be, as with all great writers, like a sixth sense, possessed and deployed with absolute confidence and ease.

The Third Miss Symons was published in 1913 and in style and tone belongs to its own day, and to the future, modern stream of English fiction. Nevertheless it looks backwards to the late Victorian era of social and feminine history, the final years of a settled, rigidly structured existence, before the Great War changed everything forever.

In the last resort, the novel has that air of timelessness possessed by all major works of art: it is artistically and humanly valid and relevant for always.

F. M. Mayor was born in 1872. She was enjoying her 30s, that first decade of true adulthood, when she wrote the novel. She, like her book, straddles the centuries. In some ways she was typical of a particular kind of educated Victorian/Edwardian spinster (with seven unmarried aunts!) yet she might also have been thought of, in her own day, as a representative of the new, emancipated woman.

Her father, a clergyman, was Emeritus Professor of Classics at King's College, London, and author of many books. Her mother was a niece of the historian George Grote. Her paternal uncle, also a parson, was Professor of Latin at Cambridge. It was to Cambridge that Flora went, to read history at Newnham, an unusual, though not by then a pioneering thing for a young woman to do at the turn of the century. A far more remarkable fact is that she went on the professional stage, with the Ben Greet company, for a time after graduating. As her niece, Lady Rothschild, writes, "Imagine at that date a clergyman's daughter from such an intransigently high-minded, classical background, doing such a thing."

Certainly it would have provided her with experience of a world far removed from that in which she had so far lived and, more important, a novel perspective on that world, and particularly on the place of the women in it. Miss Mayor was intelligent, in-dependent and enterprising, and to some degree placed herself for a time outside her own background and social position, but she was not a rebel, and when she began to write, it was about that society she had always known, the women of the provincial middle-classes in the years around the turn of the century. Henrietta "the third daughter and fifth child of Mr. and Mrs. Symons" is typical, at least in circumstances, of thousands of women of her generation and class, and the complete opposite of her creator, for she has no independence of spirit, not a trace of enterprise or individual courage. She neither seeks out opportunities nor seizes those few which come her way.

INTRODUCTION

John Masefield, in his Introduction to the first edition of the novel, described how "her brain like so many of the brains in civilization is but slightly drawn upon or exercised: she is not so much wasted as not used. Having by fortune and tradition nothing to do, she remains passive till events and time make her incapable of doing. She has done nothing but live, and been nothing but alive."

F. M. Mayor was writing about a previous generation: by her own day a few more doors had opened, at least to a young woman of her determined character. It is difficult to imagine both the claustrophobia and the enervating oppressiveness of the tedious lives Henrietta and her kind were obliged to pursue and, even more, to sympathize with a woman so depressed, so lacking in energy and spirit as to submit to its restrictions without a struggle, and with only the sort of protest that turns inward, and festers, to manifest itself merely in the form of pettiness and ill-temper.

The fault lies in Henrietta's personality as much as in her circumstances. She knows it, at least in her heart of hearts, and loathes herself, and can do nothing to escape from the prison of herself.

It is hard indeed to like her or sympathize with her, or to enjoy her company, hard not to want to give her a good shake. Yet her creator manages to write 140 pages in which there is precious little relief from her, to catalogue all her faults, to convey the impatience of her relatives and acquaintances (for she can scarcely be said to have friends) with her—and yet to view her compassionately, to awaken our understanding and sympathy, to make allowances and, finally, to redeem.

It is a profoundly sad, profoundly moving book; its ending might so easily have seemed sentimental, bathetic, or at least quite unconvincing. It is none of those things. It works, it is credible, it stirs one to tears. F. M. Mayor was a Christian, not merely because she had an upbringing in a conventionally clerical household, but because she believed in the essential tenets of the Christian faith—in love, in basic human affinity, and brotherhood, in salvation, forgiveness and compassion, and in redemption and resurrection.

We are irritated and bored by Henrietta; after her death her sister Evelyn blames herself for being neglectful and loving her too little. She says, "It was all my fault." But F. M. Mayor knows that it is the novelist's great power, and responsibility, to discern and tell the truth. And the truth is that it was not Evelyn's fault "but Henrietta's own: that it was because she was so unlovable that she was so little loved".

Yet a still greater truth follows, at a deeper level. "If she had had the chance she wouldn't have been unlovable."

The novel is the story of Henrietta's personality; its shape, the shape of her life, is a vicious circle. She becomes less and less lovable because, from the beginning of her life, she is hardly loved. Children know rejection when they meet it, and quickly assume that they are not loved because they are not worthy of love. From the opening sentence, Miss Mayor strikes a chill note; the dice are loaded against Henrietta, because of her very position in the family—"enthusiasm for babies had declined in both parents by the time she arrived".

The battle for affection and attention was over as soon as it had begun. Henrietta does have her hour. "At five, her life attained its zenith. She became a very pretty, charming little girl." But the flowering is brief enough. At eight "her charm departed never to return and she slipped back into insignificance".

What Henrietta fails to do, throughout her life, is seize the fleeting opportunity, consolidate her position and then improve upon it, whether by behaving attractively or learning to be in-gratiating. The moment things start to go wrong for her, she becomes sour and resentful, and allows her ill-temper free rein.

And sometimes the very force of her own longing for love causes her to act desperately and so lose it.

Things improve with the birth of her younger sister Evelyn and it is this relationship which is at the heart of Henrietta's life until the end, unsatisfactory in many ways though it is—for her own rudeness, tactlessness and short-temper put it under severe strain. Its culmination is unbearably poignant. At one stage, for one night, the sisters draw closer than they have been since childhood, meeting each other face to face, sharing confidences, speaking truths. After-wards Evelyn scarcely remembers it, absorbed by husband and children. To Henrietta it has been all in all. After her death, Evelyn finds a note hidden in a box. It says " 'I can't tell you how much good you have done me, I seem to have been living for this for fifteen years. Evelyn, September 23, 1890.' "

A whole life, and so little salvaged, such a morsel of affection cherished through years of loneliness, purposelessness, unhappiness.

Clearly, one of Henrietta's chief enemies is boredom, and although it is certain that other, more enterprising and robust, or else sweetly acquiescent, uncritical natures did survive the tedium and narrowness of such lives, nevertheless it was more difficult for a woman, especially a spinster, to break out.

"Even now when there is a certain amount of choice and liberty, a woman who is thrown on her own resources at thirty-nine with no previous training and no obvious claims and duties does not find it very easy to know how to dispose of herself. But a generation ago, the problem was far more difficult."

Once Henrietta's single chance of securing a husband (if a real chance it is) has been lost, she resigns herself to spinsterhood. Her sisters quickly marry, after which there are no more parties. Henrietta lingers at home, a low-spirited companion for her ailing parents, dabbling in the idea of reading Italian. After her mother's death, she housekeeps for father and brothers but she is domineering, ill-tempered, inefficient. Her father remarries, Henrietta is displaced, and the household runs smoothly and happily again, so that she realizes that "she had had her chance, her one great chance in life, and she had missed it". After that she lives mostly abroad, wandering pointlessly from one shabby-genteel pension to another, occasionally sight-seeing without any pleasure, otherwise playing patience because during a game "the clock had moved from ten minutes past eight to twenty five minutes to ten".

Her remaining years are spent in Bath, and although her daily occupations—tea parties, church affairs, the drinking of the spa waters—seem petty beyond belief, somehow she is busier and happier, and though she does not find love, she makes acquaintances, and has a loyal maid.

The days of her dying are marvellously described. Evelyn is abroad and does not receive the vital telegram which arrives too late. She discovers her sister's pathetic souvenirs, along with the note, in a little box, experiences remorse and then, suddenly, unaccountably, a mystical relevation, which is so convincing, and which redeems and transforms everything that has gone before, the whole novel, the whole of Henrietta's life, without in any way overriding or minimizing the actual "bitterness, aimlessness and emptiness" of it whilst it was being lived.

The book is an extraordinary many-faceted study of one woman, presented to us both from the eyes of its creator, and those outside of her, and at the same time from within—a complex achievement. F. M. Mayor has a devastating ability to make clear statements, generalizations that stem from innumerable minutely particular observations about human life, behaviour and society, so that we gasp at the simple enormity of what she is saying and see at once that it is the plain truth.

She is sensitive yet detached, firm and decisive in her prose style, infinitely various and subtle in her method of approach, and each reading of *The Third Miss Symons* yields up more riches. How very little material she is handling after all—and yet she is holding the whole of human life in her hand and subjecting it to scrutiny, re-creating it for us. She evinces deep sympathy and understanding. I cannot believe that anyone could read the novel without coming away from it changed, illuminated, made wiser and more understanding of its heroine and her life and times, and of the human condition in general.

Susan Hill, 1980

PREFACE

Miss Mayor's story is of a delicate quality, not common here, though occurring at intervals, and always sure of a choice, if not very large, audience among those who like in art the refined movement and the gentle line. Her subject, like her method, is one not commonly chosen by women writers; it is simply the life of an unmarried idle woman of the last generation, a life (to some eyes) of wasted leisure and deep futility, but common enough, and getting from its permitted commonness a justification from life, who is wasteful but roughly just. Miss Mayor tells this story with singular skill, more by contrast than by drama, bringing her chief character into relief against her world, as it passes in swift procession. Her tale is in a form becoming common among our best writers; it is compressed into a space about a third as long as the ordinary novel, yet form and manner are so closely suited that all is told and nothing seems slightly done, or worked with too rapid a hand. Much that is tiresome in the modern novel, the pages of analysis and of comment, the long descriptions and the nervous pathology, are omitted by Miss Mayor's method, which is all for the swift movement and against the temptations to delay which obstruct those whose eyes are not upon life; she condenses her opportunities for psychology and platitude into a couple of shrewd lines and goes on with her story, keeping her freshness and the reader's interest unabated. The method is to draw the central figure rapidly past a succession of bright lights, keeping the lights various and of many colours and allowing none of them to shine too long. This comparatively passive creative method suits the subject; for her heroine has the fate to be born in a land where myriads of women of her station go passively like poultry along all the tramways of their parishes; life is something that happens to them, it is their duty to keep to the tracks, and having enough to eat and enough to put on therewith to be content, or if not content, sour, but in any case to seek no further over the parochial bounds. Her heroine, born into such a tradition, continues in it, partly by the pressure of custom and family habit, both always very powerful and often deadly in this country, and partly from a want of illumination in herself, her instructors, and in the life about her. The latter want is the fatal defect in her: it is the national defect, " the everlasting prison remediless " into which so many thousands of our idle are yearly thrown; it is from this that she really suffers; it is to this that she succumbs, while the ivy of her disposition grows over and smothers whatever light may be in her. Like water in flood-time revolving muddily over the choked outlet, her life revolves over the evil in it without resolution or escape; her brain, like so many of the brains in civilization, is but slightly drawn upon or exercised; she is not so much wasted as not used. Having by fortune and tradition nothing to do, she remains passive till events and time make her incapable of doing, while the world glitters past in its various activity, throwing her incapacity into ever stronger relief, till her time is over and the general muddle is given a kind of sacredness, even of beauty, by ceasing. She has done nothing but live and been nothing but alive, both to such passive purpose that the ceasing is pitiful; and it is by pushing on to this end, instead of shirking it, and by marking the last tragical fact which puts a dignity upon even the meanest being, that Miss Mayor raises her story above the plane of social criticism, and keeps it sincere. A lesser writer would have been content with less, and having imagined her central figure would have continued to stick pins into it, till the result would have been no living figure, but a record of personal judgments, perhaps even, as sometimes happens, of personal pettiness, a witch's waxen figure plentifully pricked before the consuming flame. Miss Mayor keeps on the side of justice, with the real creators, to whom there is nothing simple and no one unmixed, and in this way gets beauty, and through beauty the only reality worth having.

In a land like England, where there is great wealth, little education and little general thought, people like Miss Mayor's heroine are common; we have all met not one or two but dozens of her; we know her emptiness, her tenacity, her futility, savagery and want of light; all circles contain some examples of her, all people some of her shortcomings; and judgment of her, even the isolation of her in portraiture, is dangerous, since the world does not consist of her and life needs her. In life as in art those who condemn are those who do not understand; and it is always a sign of a writer's power, that he or she keeps from direct praise or blame of imagined character. Miss Mayor arrives at an understanding of her heroine's character by looking at her through a multitude of different eyes, not as though she were her creator, but as if she were her world, looking on and happening, infinitely active and various, coming into infinite contrast, not without tragedy, but also never without fun. The world is, of course, the comparatively passive feminine world, but few modern books (if any) have treated of that world so happily, with such complete acceptance, unbiassed and unprejudiced, yet with such selective tact and variety of gaiety. She comes to the complete understanding of Henrietta by illuminating all the facets in her character and all the threads of her destiny, and this is an unusual achievement, made all the more remarkable by a brightness and quickness of mind which give delightful life to a multitude of incidents which are in themselves new to fiction. Her touch upon all her world is both swift and unerring; but the great charm of her work is its brightness and unexpectedness; it lights up so many little unsuspected corners in a world that is too plentifully curtained.

JOHN MASEFIELD, 1913

THE THIRD MISS SYMONS

CHAPTER I

HENRIETTA was the third daughter and fifth child of Mr. and Mrs. Symons, so that enthusiasm for babies had declined in both parents by the time she arrived. Still, in her first few months she was bound to be important and take up a great deal of time. When she was two, another boy was born, and she lost the honourable position of youngest. At five her life attained its zenith. She became a very pretty, charming little girl, as her two elder sisters had done before her. It was not merely that she was pretty, but she suddenly assumed an air of graciousness and dignity which captivated everyone. Some very little girls do acquire this air : what its source is no one knows. In this case certainly not Mr. and Mrs. Symons, who were particularly clumsy. Etta, as she was called, was often summoned from the nursery when visitors came ; so were Minna and Louie her elder sisters, but all the ladies wanted to talk to Etta. Minna and Louie had by this time, at nine and eleven, advanced to the ugly, uninteresting stage, and they owed Henrietta a grudge because she had annexed the petting that used to fall to them. They had their revenge in whispering interminable secrets to one another, of which Etta could hear stray sentences. " Ellen says she knows Arthur was very naughty, because . . . But we won't tell Etta." She was very susceptible to notice, and the petting was not good for her.

When she was eight her zenith was past, and her plain stage began. Her charm departed never to re⎽ ⎽, and she slipped back into insignificance. At eight she could no longer be considered a baby to play with, and a good deal of fault-finding was deemed necessary to counteract the previous spoiling. In Henrietta's youth, sixty years ago, fault-finding was administered unsparingly. She did not understand why she was more scolded than the others, and decided that it was because Ellen and Miss Weston and her mother had a spite against her.

Mrs. Symons was not fond of children, and throughout Henrietta's childhood she was delicate, so that Henrietta saw very little of her. Her chief recollections of her mother were of scoldings in the drawing-room when she had done anything specially naughty.

If she had been one of two or one of three in a present-day family she would have been more precious. But as one of four daughters—another girl was born when she was eight—she was not much wanted. Mr. Symons was a solicitor in a country town, and the problem of providing for his seven, darkened the years of childhood for the whole Symons family. The children felt that their parents found them something of a burden, and in those days there was no cult of childhood to soften the hard reality.

The two older boys had a partnership together, into which they occasionally admitted Minna and Louie. Minna and Louie had, beside their secrets, a friend named Rosa. Harold, the youngest boy, did not want any person—only toy engines. He and Etta should have been companions, but he said she cried and told tales, though she told no more tales than he did.

3

A large family should be such a specially happy community, but it sometimes occurs that there is a girl or boy who is nothing but a middle one, fitting in nowhere. So it was with Henrietta, till the youngest child was born.

Unfortunately she had an almost morbid longing, unusual in a child, to be loved and of importance. Now she would have given anything to have heard Minna and Louie's secrets, not for the sake of the secrets, but as a sign that she was thought worthy of confidence. She ran everyone's errands continually, but she broke the head off Arthur's carnation as she was bringing it from his bedroom to the garden, and she let out William's secret, which he had told her in an unusual fit of affability, in order that she might curry favour with Minna. This infuriated William, and did not conciliate Minna. She grew fast and was a little delicate. It made her irritable, but her brothers and sisters, who were all growing with great regularity, could not be expected to understand delicacy. She always said she was sorry after she had been cross, but they, who did not have tempers, could not see that that made things any better.

In her loneliness she made for herself, like many other forlorn children, a phantom friend.

4

It was a little girl two years older than she was, for Henrietta preferred to look up, and be herself in an inferior position. For this reason she did not much care for dolls, where she was decidedly the superior. She called her friend Amy. Amy slept with her, helped her with her lessons, told her secrets perpetually, and grumbled about the other children.

One day they all had a game at Hide and Seek. The lot fell on her and William, now fourteen, to hide. They ensconced themselves in a dark spot in a little grove at the end of the garden. The others could not find them, and there was plenty of time for talk. William was a kind boy and rather a chatterbox, ready to expand to any listener, even a sister of nine. Henrietta never knew how it was that she told him about Amy. It had always been her firm resolve that this was to be her own dead secret, never revealed. But the unusual warmth of the interview went to her head. It was in a kind of intoxication of happiness that she poured out her confidence. The shrubbery was so dark that William's face could not be seen, but he began fidgeting, and soon broke in : " I say, what hours the others are, it must be tea-time. Let's go and find them."

It was kind of William to snub her confidence so gently, but the disappointment was cruel. She had been lifted up to such a height of happiness. When Ellen brushed her hair at night she noticed her dismal looks, and being really concerned at Henrietta's want of control, she said bracingly that little girls must never be whiney-piney. When the lamp was put out, Henrietta sobbed herself to sleep, and she looked back on that evening as the most miserable of her childhood.

It was not long after this that the last child was born, the baby girl. They had all been sent away, and Henrietta, who had gone by herself to an aunt, came back later than the others; they had seen the new arrival, and had got over their very moderate excitement. Ellen asked Henrietta if she would like to have a peep at her little sister. When Henrietta saw it, she determined that it should be her own baby. " Oh, you little darling, you darling, darling baby !" she murmured over and over again.

" Now you are happy, aren't you, Miss Etta ?" said Ellen ; she had always felt sorry for Henrietta out in the cold.

The baby very much improved Etta's circumstances. Ellen allowed her to help, and she had something to care for, so she had less occasion for interviews with her phantom friend. As she grew older the baby Evelyn requited her affection with a gratifying preference, but she was very sweet-natured and would like everybody, and not make a party against Minna and Louie as Henrietta desired. She came to the pretty age, and was prettier and more charming than any of them. When the pretty age ought to have passed she remained as attractive as ever, and continued to enjoy a universal popularity. This was disappointing to Henrietta ; she would have preferred them to be pariahs together. Still, it was always Etta that Evelyn liked best.

When Evelyn was four and Henrietta thirteen, Evelyn was given a canary. It never became interesting, for it would not eat off her finger, but she cared for it as much as a child of four can be considered to care for anything. The canary died and was buried when Evelyn had a cold and was in bed, and Henrietta went by herself into the town, contrary to rules, and spent all her savings at a little, low bird-shop getting a mangey canary. She brought it back and put it into the cage, and when Evelyn, convalescent, came into the nursery, she attempted to palm off the new canary as Evelyn's original bird. This strange behaviour brought her to great disgrace. Her only explanation was, " I didn't want Evelyn to know that Dickie was dead. I think death is so dreadful, and I don't want her to know anything dreadful." Mrs. Symons and the governess thought this most inexplicable.

" Etta is a very difficult child," said Mrs. Symons ; " she always has been so unlike the others, and now this dreadful untruth. I always feel an untruth is very different from anything else. Going into that horrid, dirty little shop ! You must watch her most carefully, Miss Weston, and let me know if there is any further deceit."

" I never had noticed anything before, Mrs. Symons, but I will be particularly careful." And Miss Weston took the most elaborate precautions that there should be no cheating at lessons, which Henrietta resented keenly, having, like the majority of girls, an extreme horror of cheating.

CHAPTER II

Soon after the incident of the canary, the three older girls went to school. When her first home-sickness was passed, Henrietta enjoyed the life. It was strict, but home had been strict, and there was much more variety here. She was clever, and took eager delight in her lessons; dull, stupid Miss Weston had found her beyond her.

She would have liked school even more if her temper had been under better control. But at thirteen she had settled down to bad temper as a habit. She did not exactly put her feelings into thoughts, but there was an impression in her mind that as she had been out of it so much of her life she should be allowed to be bad-tempered as a consolation. This brought her into constant conflicts, which made no one so unhappy as herself.

She had two great interests at school, Miranda Hardcastle and Miss Arundel. Miranda was the kind of girl whom everybody is always going to adore, very pretty, very amusing, and with much cordiality of manner. Henrietta fell a victim at once, and Miranda, who drank in all adoration, gave Henrietta some good-natured friendship in return. Henrietta fagged for her, did as many of her lessons as she could, applauded all her remarks, amply rewarded by Miranda's welcoming smile and her, "I've been simply pining for you, my child; come and hear me my French at once, like a seraphim."

This happy state of things continued until unfortunately Henrietta's temper, over which she had kept an anxious guard in Miranda's presence, showed signs of activity. The first time this occurred Miranda opened her large eyes very wide and said, "What's come over my young friend, has it got the hydrophobia? I shall try and cure it by kindness and give it some chocolate."

Henrietta's clouds dispersed, but she was not always so easily restored to good-humour; and Miranda, with the whole school at her feet, was not going to stand bad temper, the fault on the whole least easily forgiven by girls. Henrietta had a heartrending scene with her : at fifteen she liked heartrending scenes. Miranda was too fond of popularity to give Henrietta up entirely, so the two remained friendly, but they were no longer intimate.

Miss Arundel was the head-mistress's sister, and undertook all the serious teaching that was not in the hands of masters. She did not have many outward attractions of face and form, but schoolgirls will know that that is not of much importance. She was adored, possibly because she had a bad temper (bad temper is an asset in a teacher), which was liable to burst forth unexpectedly; then she was clever and enthusiastic, and gave good lessons. She marked out Henrietta, and it came round that she had said, "Etta Symons is an interesting girl, she has possibilities. I wonder how she will turn out." It came round also that Miss Arundel had said, "I only wish she had more control and tenacity of purpose," but this sentence Henrietta put out of her head. The first sentence she thought of for hours on end, and set to work to be more interesting than ever; in fact for some days she was so affected and exasperating that Miss Arundel could hardly contain herself. Still, even Miss Arundel's sarcasm was endurable, anything was endurable, after that gratifying remark.

When Miranda ceased to be her special friend, she transferred her whole heart and soul to Miss Arundel. She waylaid her with flowers, hung about in the passage on the chance of seeing her walk by, and waited on her as much as she dared. Some teachers apparently enjoy girl adorations, and even take pains to secure them. Miss Arundel had had enough of them to find them disagreeable. She therefore gave out in the presence of two or three of Henrietta's circle that she thought it was a pity Etta Symons wasted so much of her pocket-money on buttonholes which gave very little pleasure to anyone, certainly not to her, who particularly disliked strong scents; she thought the money could be much better expended.

Jessie Winsley repeated this speech to Henrietta, little thinking what anguish it would cause. Henrietta had very little pride, very little proper pride some people might have said; she did not at all mind giving a great deal more than she got. But this speech, which was not, after all, so very malignant, drove her to despair. She went to Miranda, who hugged her, and said : " Old cat ! barbaric old cat ! Never think of her again, she isn't

12

worth it. Try dear little Stanley, he's a pet; men are much nicer." Stanley was the drawing-master.

But after all one must have a little encouragement to start an adoration, and as Henrietta never could draw, she got none from Stanley. Besides she was constant, so instead, she brooded over Miss Arundel. She had not been so unhappy, when she had her Miranda and her Arundel. Now she had lost them both. Miss Arundel, with her cool, unaffectionate interest, had, of course, never been "had" at all, but Henrietta had imagined that when Miss Arundel said "Yes, quite right, that's a good answer," it was a kind of beginning of friendship. She, Henrietta, small and insignificant, was singled out for Miss Arundel's friendship ; that was what she thought. She did not realize that it was possible to care merely for intellectual development.

When she was prepared for Confirmation, there were serious talks about her character. The Vicar, whose classes she attended, was mostly concerned with doctrines, and Mrs. Marston with what one might call a list of ideal vices and temptations which pupils must guard themselves against. Miss Arundel talked

to her about her untidy exercise books, her
unpunctuality, her loud voice in the corridor,
and her round shoulders, and explained very
properly that inattention in these comparatively
small matters showed a general want of self-
control. She did not speak about bad temper,
for Henrietta was much too frightened of her
to show any signs of temper in her proximity.
Miss Arundel did not give her an opportunity
of unburdening herself of the problem that
weighed on her mind, not that she would have
taken the opportunity if it had occurred, not
after that speech about the buttonholes. This
was the problem: Why was it that people
did not love her?—she to whom love was so
much that if she did not have it, nothing else
in the world was worth having. There had
been Evelyn, it is true, but now Evelyn did
lessons with a little friend of her own age, and
she and the friend were all in all, and did not
want Henrietta in the holidays. Henrietta re-
flected that she was not uglier, or stupider, or
duller than anyone else. There was a large set
at school who were ugly, stupid, and dull, and
they were devoted to one another, though they
none of them cared about her. Why had God
sent her into the world, if she was not wanted?

She found the problem insoluble, but a certain amount of light was thrown on it by one of the girls.

She had been snarling with two or three of her classmates over the afternoon preparation, and had flounced off in a rage by herself. She felt a touch on her arm, and turning round saw Emily Mence, a rather uncouth, clever girl, whom she hardly knew.

"I just came to say, Why *are* you such an idiot?"

"Me?"

"Yes, why do you lose your temper like that? All the girls are laughing at you; they always do when you get cross."

"Then I think it's horrid of them."

"Well, you can't be surprised; of course people won't stand you, if you're so cross."

"Won't they?" said Henrietta. "And the one thing I want in the world is to be liked."

"Do you really? Fancy wanting these girls to like you; they're such silly little things."

"I shouldn't mind that if only they liked me."

"*I* like you," said Emily. "Do you remember you said Charles I. deserved to have

15

his head cut off because he was so stupid, and all the others gushed over him ?"

" Did I ?"

" I don't like the other girls to laugh at you; that's why I thought I would tell you."

They walked up and down the path and talked about Charles I. Here there seemed the beginning of a friendship, but it was nipped in the bud, for Emily left unexpectedly at the end of the term. Henrietta received no further overtures from any of the girls.

Emily's words had made an impression however, and for six weeks Henrietta took a great deal of pains with her temper. For this concession on her part she expected Providence to give her an immediate and abundant measure of popularity. It did not. The Symons family had not the friend-making quality—a capricious quality, which withholds itself from those who have the greatest desire, and even apparently the best right, to possess it. The girls were kind, kinder, on the whole, than the grown-up world, and they were perfectly willing to give her their left arms round the garden, but their right would be occupied by their real friends, to whom they would be telling their experiences, and Henrietta would only come in for a, "Wasn't it sickening, Etta?" now and then. She was disappointed, and she relaxed her efforts. She had missed the excitement of saying disagreeable things. The day had become chilly without them. By the middle of the term she was as disagreeable as ever.

She very rarely received good advice in her life, and now that she had got it, she made no use of it. If she had, it might have changed the whole of her future. But from henceforth, on birthdays, New Year's Eves, and other anniversaries, when she took stock of herself and her character, she ignored her temper, and would not count it as a factor that could be modified. There were others as lonely as herself at school, there are always many lonely in a community; but she did not realize this, and felt herself exceptional. She imagined that she was overwhelmed with misery at this time, but really the life was so busy, and she was so fond of the lessons, and did them so well, that she was not to be pitied as much as she thought.

It was clear she was to be lonely at school and lonely at home. Where was she to find relief? There was a supply of innocuous story-books for the perusal of Mrs. Marston's pupils on Saturday half-holidays, innocuous, that is to say, but for the fact that they gave a completely erroneous view of life, and from them Henrietta discovered that heroines after the sixteenth birthday are likely to be pestered with adorers. The heroines, it is true, were exquisitely beautiful, which Henrietta knew she was not, but from a study of " Jane Eyre " and " Villette " in the holidays, Charlotte Brontë was forbidden at school owing to her excess of passion, Henrietta realized that the plain may be adored too, so she had a modest hope that when the magic season of young ladyhood arrived, a Prince Charming would come and fall in love with her. This hope filled more and more of her thoughts, and all her last term, when other girls were crying at the thought of leaving, she was counting the days to her departure.

CHAPTER III

HENRIETTA was eighteen when she left school.
Minna and Louie had gone two or three years
before, and by the time Henrietta came home,
Minna was engaged to be married. There
was nothing particular about Minna. She
was capable, and clear-headed, and rather good-
looking, and could dress well on a little money.
She was not much of a talker, but what she
said was to the point. On these qualifications
she married a barrister with most satisfactory
prospects. They were both extremely fond of
one another in a quiet way, and fond they
remained. She was disposed of satisfactorily.

Louie was prettier and more lively. She
was having a gay career of flirtations, when
Henrietta joined her. She did not at all want
a younger sister, particularly a sister with a
pretty complexion. Three years of parties
had begun to tell on her own, which was of
special delicacy. She and Henrietta had never
grown to like one another, and now there

19

went on a sort of silent war, an unnecessary war on Louie's side, for she had a much greater gift with partners than Henrietta, and her captives were not annexed.

But for her complexion there was nothing very taking in Henrietta. Whoever travels in the Tube must have seen many women with dark-brown hair, brown eyes, and too-strongly-marked eyebrows ; their features are neither good nor bad ; their whole aspect is uninterest-ing. They have no winning dimples, no speaking lines about the mouth. All that one can notice is a disappointed, somewhat peevish look in the eyes. Such was Henrietta. The fact that she had not been much wanted or appreciated hitherto began to show now she was eighteen. She was either shy and silent, or talked with too much positiveness for fear she should not be listened to ; so that though she was not a failure at dances and managed to find plenty of partners, there were none of the interesting episodes that were continually occurring on Louie's evenings, and for a year or two her hopes were not realized. The Prince Charming she was waiting for came not.

Sometimes Louie was away on visits, and

Henrietta went to dances without her. At one of these, as usual a strange young man was introduced. There was nothing special about him. They had the usual talk of first dances. Then he asked for a second, then for a third. He was introduced to her mother. She asked him to call. He came. He talked mostly to her mother, but it was clear that it was Henrietta he came to see. Another dance, another call, and meetings at friends' houses, and wherever she was he wanted to be beside her. It was an exquisitely happy month. He was a commonplace young man, but what did that matter? There was nothing in Henrietta to attract anyone very superior. And perhaps she loved him all the more because he was not soaring high above her, like all her previous divinities, but walking side by side with her. Yes, she loved him; by the time he had asked her for the third dance she loved him. She did not think much of his proposing, of their marrying, just that someone cared for her. At first she could not believe it, but by the end of the month the signs clearly resembled those of Louie's young men. Flowers, a note about a book he had lent her, a note about a mistake he had made in his last note; she was sure he must care for her. The other girls at the dances noticed his devotion, and asked Henrietta when it was to be announced. She laughed off their questions, but they gave her a thrill of delight. All must be well.

And if they had married all would have been well. There might have been jars and rubs, with Henrietta's jealous disposition there probably would have been, but they would have been as happy as the majority of married couples; she would have been happier, for to many people, even to some women, it is not, as it was to her, the all-sufficing condition of existence to love and be loved.

At the end of the month Louie came home. Henrietta had dreaded her return. She had no confidence in herself when Louie was by. Louie made her cold and awkward. She would have liked to have asked her not to come into the room when he called, but she was too shy; there had never been any intimacy between the sisters. Mrs. Symons however, spoke to Louie. "A very nice young fellow, with perfectly good connections, not making much yet, but sufficient for a start. It would do very well."

Louie would not have considered herself

more heartless than other people, but she was a coquette, and she did not want Henrietta to be settled before her. The next time the young man came, he found in the drawing-room not merely a very much prettier Miss Symons, that in itself was not of much consequence, but a Miss Symons who was well aware of her advantages, and knew moreover from successful practice exactly how to rouse a desire for pursuit in the ordinary young man.

Henrietta saw at once, though she fought hard, that she had no chance.

"Are you going to the Humphreys to-morrow?" he said to Louie.

"If Henrietta's crinoline will leave any room in the carriage," answered Louie, "I shall try to get a little corner, perhaps under the seat, or one could always run behind. I crushed—see, what did I crush?—a little teeny-tiny piece of flounce one terrible evening; didn't I, Henrietta? And I was never allowed to hear the last of it."

She smiled a special smile, only given to the most favoured of her partners. The young man thought how pretty this sisterly teasing was on the part of the lovely Miss Symons; Henrietta saw it in another light.

"My crinolines are not larger than yours, you know they are not."

"Methinks the lady doth protest too much, don't you, Mr. Dockerell?"

"And you always take the best seat in the carriage, so it is nonsense to say . . ."

He noticed for the first time how loud her voice was.

"Please let us change the conversation," said Louie gently, "it can't be at all interesting for Mr. Dockerell. I am ready to own anything you like, that you don't wear crinolines at all, if that will please you."

"If there is any difficulty, could not my mother take one of you to-morrow night?" (It was Louie he looked at.) "She is staying with me for a week. Couldn't we call for you? It would be a great pleasure."

"Oh, thank you," began Henrietta.

"Really," said Louie, "you make me quite ashamed of my poor little joke. I don't think we have come quite to such a state of things that two sisters can't sit in the same carriage. I hear you are a most alarmingly good archer, Mr. Dockerell, and I want to ask you to advise me about my bow, if you will be so kind." To be asked advice, of course, completed the conquest.

Mr. Dockerell had not been so much in love with Etta as with marrying. It took him a very short time to change, but when he had made his offer and Louie had discovered that he was too dull a young man for her, he did not transfer his affections back to Henrietta. She would gladly have taken him if he had. He left the neighbourhood, and not long after married someone else.

In this grievous trouble Henrietta did not know where to turn for comfort. Mrs. Symons was one of those women who are much more a wife than a mother. She could enter into all Mr. Symons' feelings quite remarkably, even his most out-of-the-way masculine feelings, but her daughters, who on the whole were very ordinary young women, she did not understand. Perhaps Henrietta was not altogether ordinary, but after all it is not exceptional to want to be loved. Nor did Mrs. Symons care particularly for her daughters; she liked her sons much better, she would perhaps have been happier without daughters; and she liked Henrietta the least, connecting her still with those disagreeable childish interviews when Henrietta had been brought down, black and sulky, to be scolded.

Henrietta was now passing through what is not an extraordinary experience in a woman's life. She had loved and been loved, and then had been disappointed. Her mother in her distress was no more comfort than, I was going to say, the servants, but she was much less, for Ellen, now Mrs. Symons' maid, gave poor Henrietta some of the sympathy for which she hungered.

Evelyn was away, her parents had consented to her being educated with the little friend abroad, and if she had been at home, she was only fourteen, too young to be of much use. However Henrietta poured out her bitterness to her in a long letter, and Evelyn wrote back full of loving sentiment and sentimentality. Henrietta wrote also to Miranda, and had a sympathetic letter in answer, most sympathetic, considering that Miranda had just consummated a triumphant engagement to the son of an earl.

Mrs. Symons could not help thinking that Henrietta had stupidly muddled her affairs, and wasted the good chance which had been contrived for her. This was the view she presented to her husband, so that though they tried not to show it in their manner, they both felt a little aggrieved.

26

It was to William that she turned, though she remembered clearly the disappointing interview of her childhood. William, now a solicitor in London, came home for a few days' holiday. The Sunday of his visit was wet. When Mr. and Mrs. Symons were both asleep in the drawing-room, he and Henrietta sat in the former school-room, and kept up friendly small-talk about the neighbourhood. There was something so solid and comfortable about his face that she felt she must tell him. She wanted to lean on someone; she had not, she never had, any satisfaction, any pride in battling for herself. Yet she knew that William's face was deceptive; it would be much better not to speak. She determined, therefore, that she would say very little, and speak as coolly as she could. She began, but before she could stop herself, the whole story was out, and much more than the story, unbridled abuse of Louie, who was William's favourite sister. She only stopped at last, because her sobs made it impossible to speak.

"It does seem unlucky," said William, "very unlucky. I should talk it over with mother."

"Mother thinks it was my own fault. I know she does."

"Well—um—write to Minna; yes, you might write to Minna."

"Minna is only interested in the baby. She hardly ever writes; besides, she never cared about me at all. She would be glad."

"Oh, well, I shouldn't think it was worth while taking it to heart. Just go out to plenty of dances and be jolly; you mustn't mope. If you can get Aunt Mercer to give you a bed, I'll take you to the play. That will do you all the good in the world."

"It's very kind of you, William."

"Oh, that's all right. Well," going to the window, "it's no good staying in all the afternoon, it makes one so hipped. I shall take a turn and look in on Beardsley on my way back. Tell mother not to wait supper for me."

She knew she had better have said nothing. He hated the recesses of the heart being revealed, particularly those special recesses of a woman's heart; he had thought her unmaidenly. But he was sorry for her; he took her to the play, a rousing farce, for he was one of those who naively consider that two hours of laughing can compensate for months of misery, and even be a remedy. He gave

28

her a brooch also, and said to his mother, " I think Etta gets low by herself, now Minna is married and Louie is away. Why shouldn't she go for some visits?"

It may seem strange that Henrietta should have spread broadcast a grief which most people would keep hidden in their own hearts. But it is one of the saddest things about lonely people, that, having no proper confidant, they tell to all and sundry what ought never to be told to more than one. When, however, the overmastering desire for sympathy had passed, words cannot express her regret that she had spoken. For years and years afterwards it would suddenly come upon her, " I told him and he despised me," and she would beat her foot on the floor with all her might, in a useless transport of remorse.

Both Louie and Henrietta had felt it was wiser not to see too much of one another after Mr. Dockerell's proposal. Louie had gone away for a month or six weeks, and when she came back, Henrietta went for a long visit to Minna.

With two babies, the youngest very delicate, Minna was completely absorbed. She was emphatically Mrs. Willard now, not Minna

Symons. Mrs. Symons had told her something of Henrietta's circumstances, and Minna considered that the best balm would be her babies. So they might have been for people with a natural admiration for babies, but this Henrietta had not got. If Minna's children had been neglected she would have loved them dearly, but when they were surrounded by the jealous care of mother, nurse, nursemaid, and (if any space was left for him) father, there was nothing for her but to look on as an outsider.

It was during this visit that she heard of the young man's engagement. She did not realize, till she heard, how tightly she had been clinging to the hope that he might come back. Close following on that came the news that Louie was engaged to a most amiable and agreeable colonel. This made her more bitter, if it was possible to be more bitter, against Louie than before. Louie was not merely let off scot-free for what she did, but was to have every happiness given to her. Why? The old problem of her Confirmation year pressed itself on her, only now she felt less mournful and more acrid.

Her troubles made her peevish and disagreeable, as was apparent from Minna's kindly admonition.

" I think," said she, as they sat sewing one morning, " that I really ought to warn you not to talk quite so loud and so positively. I don't like saying anything, but of course I am older than you, and that is the sort of thing that spoils a girl's chances. Men don't like it. And your temper—even Arthur noticed it, and he is not at all an observant man. I daresay you hardly realize the importance of a good temper, Etta, but in my opinion it makes more difference in life than anything else."

Henrietta came back three days before Louie's wedding. Louie repented the injury she had done, and on the last night she came into Henrietta's room and apologized. " You know, Etty, I am very sorry, very, very sorry. Of course I had no idea how you felt about him. He wasn't the sort of man one could take very seriously, at least that was what I thought. Anyhow I wouldn't worry about it any more, for you know I think he cannot have been very seriously touched, or he would have made some effort to see you again, surely, after his little episode with me."

Louie felt more than her words conveyed,

but she could not demean herself to show too much.

"Perhaps you didn't mean it unkindly," said Henrietta; "I shall try to believe you, but you've wrecked my life."

"Etta is so exaggerated and hysterical," said Louie afterwards, talking things over. But as a matter of fact Henrietta spoke only the sober truth.

CHAPTER IV

AFTER Louie's wedding Henrietta went to
stay with an aunt, her father's eldest sister,
almost a generation older than he was. She
lived in a little white house in the country,
with a green verandah and French windows.
She was a kind, nice old lady, not well off, a
humble great-aunt to the whole village.
Children continually came to eat her mul-
berries; girls were found places; sick people
were sent jelly, and there was always a
great deal of sewing and knitting for poor
friends.

She did her best to make the visit pass
cheerfully; she had some little scheme of
pleasure for each day, and so many people
came and went that, though not exciting, the
life could not possibly be called dull.

Henrietta did not know whether Mrs.
Symons had mentioned her trouble to her
aunt; she hoped not. Now that the first shock
was over, she had become sensitive on the

subject, and did not wish to speak about it. From a little speech her aunt made, it is possible that Mrs. Symons had said something.

One day as they sat talking comfortably and confidentially over the fire, the conversation turned on her aunt's past days. She had been left motherless, the eldest of a large family, when she was nineteen or twenty. It was evidently her duty to devote herself to the younger ones, and when a man presented himself whom she loved and by whom she was loved, she felt that she could not be spared from home.

Henrietta saw that she was bracing herself to say something. At last out it came:

" You know, my dear, I think in spite of— I mean that there are many things besides— though when one has hoped—still life can be very happy, very peaceful, without. Why, there is this garden, and there are those three darling little children next door."

Henrietta knew that this unanalysable sentence was meant to comfort her. She felt grateful, but she was not comforted. Her aunt's life was the sweetest and happiest possible for old age, but could she at twenty settle down to devising treats for other people's children, or sewing garments for the poor? It made her feel sick and dismal to think of it. Besides, their circumstances were not similar. Her aunt, fortified by the spirit of self-sacrifice, had resigned what she loved, but she had the reward of being the most necessary member of her circle. Henrietta had had no scope for self-sacrifice, for she had never had anything to give up. In fact she envied her aunt, for she realized now that Mr. Dockerell could never have cared for her. And far from being the most necessary member of her family, her difficulty was to squeeze into a place at all.

The visit came to an end. She went home, and regular life began again. Since one ordinary young man had been attracted to her when she was twenty, there seemed no reason why other ordinary men should not continue to be attracted. As he had been in love with marrying rather than with her, so she had been in love with being loved rather than with him. She would have accepted almost any pleasant young man, provided he had had the supreme merit of caring for her. But the inscrutable fate which rules these matters, decreed that it was not to be.   No other suitor presented himself.

For one thing, she went to fewer parties now.   After Louie's marriage, Mrs. Symons, who had worked hard in the good cause of finding husbands, began to flag.   Henrietta was not so gratifying to take out as Louie had been, particularly as her complexion went off early, and without her complexion she had nothing to fall back on.   So Mrs. Symons gave herself up to the luxury of bad health, and said she could not stand late hours. When Henrietta did go out, her experience made her feel that she was unlikely to please; and though no one can define what produces attractiveness, it is safe to say that one of the most necessary elements is to believe oneself attractive.

Mr. Symons had not hitherto taken great interest in his daughters, but when Minna and Louie were married, he became fonder of them.   He was one of those men whose good opinion of a woman is much strengthened if confirmed by another man.   His daughters' husbands had confirmed his opinion in the most satisfactory way by marrying them, whereas his good opinion of Henrietta, far from being confirmed, had been rather weakened. Minna and Louie's virtues, husbands, and houses were often extolled now, and there was nothing to extol in her. Henrietta felt this continually. Her parents did not speak to her of her misfortunes; she was left alone, which is perhaps what most girls would have liked best. Not so Henrietta.

The three years after Louie's marriage were the most miserable of Henrietta's life. If she did not go out to parties, what was she to do? The housekeeping? The housekeeping, as in many cases, was not nearly enough to provide her mother with occupation. It certainly could not be divided into occupation for two. Nursing her mother? Her mother much preferred that Ellen, on whom she had become very dependent, should do what was necessary, and for companionship she had all she wanted in her husband. He was away for several hours in the day however, and during his absence Henrietta did drive out with her mother, read to her, and sit with her, and as they were so much together and shared the small events of the country town, they were to a certain extent drawn together. But Mrs. Symons always treated Henrietta *de haut en*

bas, and snubbed her when she thought necessary, as if she had been a child of ten, so that
Henrietta was constrained and a little timid
with her. There was the suggestion of a feeling that Mrs. Symons was to be pitied for
having Henrietta still on her hands. If
Henrietta had refused to be snubbed, there
would have been none of that suggestion.
Evelyn was still away at school. There were
a certain number of girls of Henrietta's age
whom she saw from time to time, but as her
mother did not wish to be disturbed by entertaining, they were not asked to the house, and
therefore did not ask Henrietta to theirs.
Besides, she was sensitive, thinking, truly, that
they were discussing her misfortune, and did
not want to see them.

In addition to the poignancy of disappointment, of present dulness and aimlessness,
Henrietta realized forcibly, though perhaps not
forcibly enough for the truth, that the years
between eighteen and thirty were her marrying years, which, slowly as they passed from
the point of view of her happiness, went only
too fast, when she considered that once gone
they could never come back, and that as they
fled, they took her chances with them.

Fifty years ago the large majority of the girls of her class married early, and the years of home life after school were arranged on the supposition that they were a short period of preparation for marriage. It did not matter to Minna and Louie that they had no interests to fill their days, that their life had been nothing but parties and intervals of waiting for parties, because it had only lasted four or five years. It had done what it was intended to do, it had settled them very comfortably with husbands. But with Henrietta, the condition which was meant to be temporary, seemed spreading itself out to be permanent, and with the parties taken away, she was hard put to it to fill up her days. She longed inexpressibly for school, for its restrictions, its monotony and variety. And to think that when she had the luck to be there, she had counted the days to being a young lady. When she remembered how she had almost wept at Miss Arundel's description of Joan of Arc, her mouth watered for lessons. As for Miss Arundel herself, she hungered and thirsted after her.

At last she had a happy thought; she decided that she would read Italian, read Dante. Miss Arundel had taught her Italian, and she would write to Miss Arundel, and ask her to recommend a good translation. She remembered that Miss Arundel and Mrs. Marston had occasionally had favourite old pupils to stay with them. She imagined how one letter might lead to another, and how at last Miss Arundel might invite her to stay too. She wrote her letter with great care and great delight, constantly changing her words, for none seemed good enough for Miss Arundel, and making a fair copy, as if it were an exercise to be sent up for correction.

Miss Arundel received the letter, read it through, came to the signature, and could not for the life of her remember who Henrietta Symons was. So many girls had passed through her hands, and she lived in the present rather than the past. A teacher was ill, she was very busy, the letter slipped her memory. One evening it came into her head, and she asked her sister, " By the by, who was Henrietta Symons ?"

" I recollect the name perfectly," said Mrs. Marston. " Let me see ; yes, now I know. There were three of them, one was Minnie, I believe, and I think Etta had a bad headache at the picnic. It was a blazing day that year, the hottest I ever remember, and I had to come back early with her."

"Of course; I remember now," said Miss Arundel. "A girl with very marked eyebrows." And she wrote back a postcard, "Tr. of D.'s D. C. Carey, 2 vols., Ward and Linsell. M. Arundel."

The postcard made Henrietta inclined to back out of Dante. But by this time she had arranged to read with a neighbour, Carrie Bostock, so she had to make a start. They did start, but as they neither understood the Italian, nor the translation, nor the notes, they found continual excuses for not reading, till Carrie boldly suggested "I Promessi Sposi," which went much better. They did not read for long, however, for Carrie became engaged, it seemed to Henrietta that everybody she knew was becoming engaged, and Carrie considered her engagement an occupation which gave her no time for anything else, certainly no time for Italian.

Henrietta found she did not read by herself. The two years away from school made it difficult to start. Perhaps it may seem strange that a girl who had been so eager at school, should not care to work by herself at home.

But when there are no competitors and no Miss Arundel, work loses much of its zest for everyone except the real student, who is rarely to be found among men, still more rarely among women. And the last thing Henrietta would ever be was unusual.

Clever, interesting schoolgirls are not at all uncommon, though not so general as clever, interesting children. But there are few who remain clever and interesting when they grow up. Uninspiring surroundings, and contact with life, or mere accumalation of years, take something away. Or perhaps it simply is that when they are grown up they are judged by a more severe standard. Miss Arundel had been disappointed again and again. But she would not have been surprised that Henrietta let everything go, for she had always observed in her an unfortunate strain of weakness.

Besides being weak, Henrietta was always affected by the people she was with, and the atmosphere of home life was not encouraging to study. "Reading Italian, my dear?" her mother would say. "Oh, can't you find anything better to do than that? Surely there must be some mending;" while her father advised her, through her mother, "not to become too clever;

it was a great pity for a girl to get too clever."

After all, there seemed no earthly reason why she should read Italian; it gave no pleasure to herself or to anyone else. So she spent most of the long leisure hours sitting by the window and thinking. She often said to herself the verse of a poem then just published by Christina Rossetti. She had seen it on a visit, copied it out, and learned it:

> "Downstairs I laugh and sport and jest with all,
>   But in my solitary room above
> I turn my face in silence to the wall:
>   My heart is breaking for a little love."

It did not quite apply to Henrietta, for she was not sporting and jesting downstairs with anyone, but that verse was the greatest comfort to her of those dreary years. The writer *must* have been through it all, she thought; she knows what it is. Not to be alone, to have someone, though an unknown one, who could share it, lightened her burden, when she was in a mood that it should be lightened.

She made up verses too, and wrote them in a pretty album she bought for the purpose. They relieved her heart a little—at any rate it was a distraction to think of the rhymes. She would have shown them to Carrie, if she had had the slightest encouragement, but as Carrie gave no encouragement, there was no one to see them.

> "While Nature op'ed her lavish hand
> And fairest flowers displayed,
> 'Twas his to taste of sunny joys,
> 'Twas mine to sit in shade.

> " Oh, talk not to me of a lasting devotion !
> It shrivels, it ceases, it fades and it dies.
> In the heart of a man 'tis a fleeting emotion ;
> Alas, in a woman eternal it lies !"

A poet would have said that anyone capable of writing that was incapable of feeling, but he would have been wrong.

Sometimes Henrietta used to have a phantom lover like the phantom friend of her childhood, but now—had she more or less imagination as a child?—she could not bear it. She imagined the phantom, and then she wanted him so intensely that she had to forget him. The aspect of certain days would be connected with some peculiarly mournful moments. She wondered which was the most depressing, the dark setting in at four o'clock and leaving her seven hours of drawing-room fancy work (for it disturbed her mother if she went to bed before eleven), or the summer sun that would not go down.

If only some kind stroke of misfortune had taken away all Mr. Symons' money. Disagreeable poverty would have been a great comfort to her. She would have been forced to make an effort; not to brood and concentrate herself on her misery. But Mr. Symons, on the contrary, continued to get richer, and throughout her fairly long, dull life, Henrietta was always cursed with her tidy little income.

But interminable as the time seemed, it passed. It passed, so that reading her old journal with the record of her happy month, she found that it had all happened five years ago, and was beginning to be forgotten. She felt as if it had not happened to her, but to some ordinary girl who had ordinary prosperity. At the same time her lot did not seem so bitter as it had done; she had become used to it. Though she herself hardly realized it, and certainly could not have said when the change had come, she was not now particularly unhappy. It was an alleviation that her mother was more of an invalid, so that some of the responsibilities of the household devolved on her, and her mother leaned on her a little. She was certainly not the prop of the house, or the lodestar to which they all turned for guidance, none of the satisfactory things women are called in poetry, but she was not such an odd-man-out as she had been.

CHAPTER V

AND now the even course of Henrietta's life was interrupted. Evelyn returned home. She and her friend were both grown up into young ladies. Many letters had passed between the sisters, but it was so long since they had seen one another that each felt a little shy at the meeting.

Evelyn was very lovely, made to please and be pleased, a regular mid-Victorian heroine, universally courted. Though always courted she was never spoilt, and was a most affectionate sister and daughter. But the old particular bond which had attached her and Henrietta no longer existed. She was equally affectionate to Minna and Louie.

Still, her coming made a great difference to Henrietta. There was a person of her own generation and way of thinking to converse with; they could have jokes together, and Evelyn was still full of schoolgirl enthusiasm. She had numberless schemes of occupation,

duets, French readings, and splashwork. And
when she went away on visits, there were her
letters, much more intimate than those of a
year or two earlier, full of allusions to their
new occupations, and teazing of a kind, compli-
mentary sort, which was new and very delightful to Henrietta.

They were arranging flowers in the school-
room one afternoon, roses which had been brought
to Evelyn by an admirer. They dropped some
on the floor, both stooped to pick them up, and
they knocked their heads together. Evelyn got
up laughing, but felt her hand suddenly snatched,
and kissed with a long, eager kiss. She turned
round, startled. "What is it ?" she said.

"I couldn't help it," said Henrietta, half
hysterically. "If you knew what it is to me
to have you back. I can't tell you."

"Is it, dear ?" said Evelyn. "I'm so glad."
And she smoothed Henrietta's forehead with a
pretty gesture full of sweetness, but with a
touch of condescension in it. She had listened
already to so many passionate declarations
about herself (one that very afternoon) that she
was not so much impressed by Henrietta's as
most younger sisters would have been. Still
she could not help contrasting herself in her

48

triumphant youth with Henrietta, disregarded
by everyone and snubbed,. Mr. and Mrs.
Symons never snubbed Evelyn, and she
thought for a moment, " Oh, I'm thankful I'm
not her"; but she put the thought away as
unkind, and supposed vaguely that Henrietta
was so good she did not mind.

Now that Evelyn was come back, Mrs.
Symons roused herself from her invalidism to
provide amusements for her. So little was
possible at home that almost at once a round
of gay visits was arranged. Minna was less
engrossed now that the babies were older, and
took her out to parties; and Louie had all the
officers of her husband's regiment at command.
These same attractions had been offered to
Henrietta. Louie had been most sincerely
anxious to atone for the past, and had invited
her again and again, but Henrietta had always
refused; for though the original wound was
healed, she still cherished resentment against
Louie.

Evelyn's was a career of triumph. Her
letters, and Louie's and Minna's were full of
officers and parties. This roused Henrietta's
old discontent. Why was Evelyn to have
everything and she nothing ? She promptly

answered herself, " Because Evelyn is so sweet and beautiful, she deserves everything she can get." But the question refused to be snubbed, and asked itself again. She hated herself for envying, and continued to envy.

Evelyn came home from her visits very much excited and interested about herself, but still not unmindful of Henrietta.

" Let me come in to your room, Etty, and tell you everything. I had a perfect time with Louie; she was a dear. She was always saying, ' Now, who shall we have to dinner? You must settle;' so I just gave the word, and whoever I wanted was produced. Louie wishes you would go too. Do go, you would have such fun. She gave me a note for you."

" My dear Etta," the note ran,

" The 9th is having a dance on the 28th. I wish you would come and stay with us for it. Come, and bring Evelyn. I particularly want to have her for it. There is a special reason. Everyone is enchanted with the dear little thing. I shall be disappointed if you don't come too. It all happened such years ago, surely we may forget it; and Edward is always asking me why I do not have you, and it seems so absurd, when I have no proper reason to give. I shall really think it too bad of you, if you don't come.

Your affec.,
L. N. CARRINGTON."

Henrietta, thinking over the matter, found there was no reason why she should not go. At twenty-seven she felt herself rather older than this generation at forty-eight, and thought it ridiculous that she should be going to a dance. But once she was there, Louie made her feel so much at home, she found her remarks were so warmly welcomed, and her few hesitating sallies so much enjoyed, that she began to think that after all she was not completely on the shelf.

"Don't go to-morrow, Etta—stay here. There's the Steeplechase on Friday; I want you to see that."

"No, thank you, Louie," said Henrietta; "I can't leave mother longer. It's been very delightful, more delightful than you can realize, perhaps—you're so much accustomed to it; but I must get back."

"Now, that really is nonsense, Etta. Mother

has Ellen, and she has father, and she is pretty well for her; you said so yourself."

But Henrietta persisted in her refusal, for she had all the strong, though sometimes unthinking, sense of duty of her generation.

"Well, if you will go, you must. But now you have begun coming, come often. Write a line whenever you like and propose yourself."

As they said good-night, Louie whispered, "Have you forgiven me, Etty?"

"Yes," said Henrietta, "that's all past and gone."

"For a matter of fact," said Louie, "he is not very happy with her; they don't get on. The Moffats know him, and Mrs. Moffat told me."

"Oh, I am sorry," said Henrietta, but she was not displeased.

Evelyn stayed behind, and Louie talked Henrietta over with her. "Poor," ever since her marriage Henrietta had been "poor" to Louie, "Poor Etta really isn't bad-looking, and when she gets animated she isn't unattractive. If I could have her here often, I believe I could do something for her."

When Evelyn came home a week or so later, she had an announcement to make. She had become engaged to an officer, a friend of the Carringtons, who had been staying in the house. He was delightful, the engagement was everything that was to be desired, and Evelyn was radiant.

Henrietta knew that such an announcement was bound to come sooner or later, but she had so longed for a few years' happy intercourse together. She tried to think only of Evelyn, but she could not keep back all that was in her mind.

"Think of me left all alone. It was so dreary, and when you came you made everything different. Now it will go back to what it was before."

"No, no, Etty darling; you will come and stay with us for months and months."

"No, I shan't. When you have got him you won't want me."

"Yes, I shall. I shall want you all the more. I love you more than I've ever done in my life, my darling sister. We've always been special, we two, haven't we, ever since I can remember?"

Henrietta was a little comforted, and did not realize that though Evelyn's tenderness was absolutely sincere, it came from the strange expansion of the heart which accompanies true love, and was not habitual.

The marriage took place almost at once, for the Captain's regiment was ordered on foreign service, and Evelyn went away to regions where it was not possible for Henrietta to visit her.

But if she had lived in England, Henrietta would not have felt herself at liberty to go away for long. After she got home, she felt glad she had not extended her visit to the Carringtons, for Mrs. Symons was not so well, and she died shortly afterwards, and Henrietta reigned in her stead.

CHAPTER VI

THE household changed now; two new elements were introduced : William came from London to be a partner in his father's firm, and lived at home, and Harold, who had been employed by an engineer in the North, found work in the neighbourhood and came back too. So that Henrietta's life became at once much fuller of interest and importance than it had been for years. As the only lady of the house, she was bound to be considered, to make decisions, to have much authority in her own hands, and at twenty-seven she greatly appreciated authority. If she was not to have love, she would at any rate have position, and the servants found her an exacting mistress. Mrs. Symons, though she had given over certain duties to Henrietta, had kept herself head of the house to the time of her death. She had a way with servants : they always liked her, and stayed with her ; but latterly she had let things slide, and when Henrietta took her

place she found much to criticize. Most of
the servants left, but some stayed, and agreed
with Ellen that it was "just Miss Henrietta's
way; she was funny sometimes." However,
they got used to her, and things jogged along
pretty quietly.

When Ellen left to be married, and there
was no one in the kitchen to make allowances
for her, she had much more difficulty, and
Mr. Symons was occasionally disturbed in his
comfortable library by an indignant apparition,
which declared amid gulps that it had "no
wish whatever to make complaints, but really
Miss Henrietta —— !"

Mr. Symons thought this very hard.
"Can't you manage to make them decently
contented? We never used to have this sort
of thing," he would say. Henrietta would
defend herself by counter-charges, and on the
whole felt the incident was creditable to her,
as showing that she was a power, and a rather
dreaded power, in the house.

The men thought also that they were under
a needlessly harsh yoke. Henrietta grumbled
when they were late for meals, or creased the
chintzes, or let the dog in with muddy paws.
From a combination of kindness, weakness,

and letting things slide, they made no complaints. Mr. Symons always remembered and felt sorry for the episode which Henrietta herself had almost forgotten, and he was determined to make up to her by letting her be as unpleasant as she liked at home.

If only they had spoken strongly while there was yet time. They did not realize, it is difficult for those in the same house to realize, where things were tending. Henrietta's temper became less violent; there are fewer occasions for losing a temper when one is grown up, but she took to nagging like a duck to water.

But if they made no complaints, the men left her to herself. Mr. Symons spent many hours at his club, and her brothers entertained their friends in the smoking-room. She was vaguely disappointed ; she had an idea, gleaned from novels and magazines, that as the home daughter to a widowed father, the home sister to two brothers, she would be consulted, leant on, confided in. Mr. Symons missed his wife at every turn, but he never felt Henrietta could take her place. Her nagging shut up his heart against her. He thought it silly, rather unfairly, perhaps, for she inherited the habit from her mother, and he had never thought *her* nagging silly.

As to William and Harold, they had come to the ages of thirty-five and twenty-six without any wish for confidence, and why should they wish to confide in Henrietta? She was not wise and she was not sympathetic. The mere fact that they lived in the same house with her caused no automatic opening of the heart. Well on in middle life, William became engaged, and suddenly poured out everything to his love, but for the present he and Harold were content to go through life never saying anything about themselves to anybody. In fact, they hardly ever thought of Henrietta. She would have been astonished if she had known what an infinitesimal difference she made in their lives.

As mistress of the house, Henrietta was promoted to the circle of the married ladies, and the happiest hours of her life were spent in visits she and they interchanged, when they talked about servants, arrangements, prices, and health.

They were not intimate friends. Perhaps the women of fifty years ago did not have the faculty of staunch and close friend-making

possessed by our generation. And now
Henrietta did not very much want to make
friends. She would have thought intimacy a
little schoolgirlish, a little beneath a middle-
aged lady's dignity.

Her parents had been a very ordinary couple
in a country town. They and the society they
frequented were uncultivated, and uninterested
in everything that was going on in the world
outside. The men, of course, were occupied
with their professions, and almost all the ladies
had large growing families, which gave full
scope for their energies. Henrietta had not
their duties, and was better off than the
majority of them, but she did not find time
hang heavy on her hands. Long ere this she
had learnt the art of getting through the day
with the minimum of employment. Now, of
course, her various duties gave her a certain
amount to do, but not enough to occupy her
mind profitably. She often said, " I am so
busy I really haven't a moment to spare," and
quite sincerely declined the charge of a district,
because she had no time. If any visitors were
coming to stay, she spoke of the preparations
and the work they entailed, as if all was per-
formed by her single pair of hands. " What

with Louie and Edward coming to-morrow,
and Harold going to the Tyrol on Wednesday,
I cannot think how I shall manage, but I
suppose," with a resigned smile, "I shall
get through somehow." She was persuaded
into visiting a small hospital once a fortnight
for an hour, and the day and hour were much
dreaded by her entourage, so vastly did they
loom on the horizon, and so submissively must
every other event wait on their convenience.

Minna and Louie often came on visits with
their children. The three sisters got on much
better than formerly, though Minna and Louie
were both two much absorbed in their own
interests to give Henrietta a large place in
their thoughts. Minna's husband failed early
in health, before he had had time to fulfil his
promising early prospects, while Louie's Colonel,
when he retired from the army, occupied his
leisure in speculation, and greatly diminished
that attractive fortune of his. All three sisters
had a certain amount of money left to them by
their mother, but in spite of this Minna and
Louie were now both, comparatively speaking,
poor, while Henrietta, with no one dependent
on her, and a large allowance from her father, was
comfortably off. Louie and Minna quite gave

up talking of " poor Henrietta," and " Really Henrietta has done very well for herself," was a remark frequently exchanged.

Henrietta had always been generous, and her sisters soon came to expect as a right that she should rescue them in times of domestic need : pay for a nephew's schooling, send a delicate niece to the sea, and give very substantial presents at birthdays and Christmas. Their point of view seemed to be that if anyone had been so lucky as to keep out of the bothers of marriage, the least she could do was to help her unfortunate sisters. Still, they disliked being beholden to Henrietta, and, half intentionally, set their children against her to relieve their feelings. The children were not bad children, but Henrietta found their visits burdensome. She was becoming a little set and unwilling to be disturbed, and she said the children were spoilt. Minna and Louie had determined they would not be the strict parents of the elder generation, whereas Henrietta, who remembered all the snubbing of her youth, wanted to have her turn of giving snubs, and this did not make her popular. She never grew very fond of these children, but kept her affection for something else.

61

For it is not to be supposed that a heart with such peculiar longing for love was to be satisfied with a life in which feeling played so little part. She had put aside the desire for a lover now. She was not one of the women whom nothing will satisfy but marriage; on the whole she did not care very much for men. She wanted what she had always wanted, something to love and something to love her. And she had good reason to hope that at last that wish might be realized, for it was agreed between her and Evelyn that if there were any children, she was to bring them up while Evelyn was abroad. Round this hope she built many happy schemes.

Henrietta had seen very little of Evelyn all this time—the regiment went from one foreign station to another—but very affectionate letters passed between the two.

For some years no children were born. Then came a little girl. "She is to be called Etta," said Evelyn's letter, "and you know she is your baby as well as ours. Do you remember what you did for me in old days? I think of how you will do the same for baby, and I could not bear for anyone else to do it but you." The baby died in the first year.

Then came a little boy, who lived an even shorter time; then another little girl. The parents and Henrietta hardly dared to hope this time. But the perilous first year passed, then, although she was always very delicate, a second, third, and fourth. Then, when the plans were maturing for her coming home, she died too. It seems sometimes as if Death cannot leave a certain family alone, but comes back to it again and again.

"Evelyn is broken-hearted," her husband wrote, "and if she stays in this horrible India I believe I shall lose her too. I am going to exchange if I can to a home regiment, or I shall leave the army. I do not care what we do as long as I get her away. In the midst of it all she keeps thinking of how you will feel it. I believe a good cry with you is the one thing that might comfort her."

Henrietta took this letter to her father, and implored him to let her go out to India at once. But this Mr. Symons, though kind and sympathetic and truly sorry for Evelyn, could not bring himself to allow. He was getting to the age when he shrank from violent upheavals. Herbert said they were leaving India. By the time she arrived they would probably be gone, and then what a wild goose chase it would be. Then, of course, she could not go alone, and who was to go with her? Her brothers could not spare the time, and he did not feel up to going, and she must have a man with her. Edward? No, certainly not. Since his speculations, Edward was in bad odour. No, it would be much better to write a kind letter—he would write too—and drop this really foolish scheme, which would, among other things, be very costly, more costly then he felt prepared to face just then.

She said she would go alone.

"Then you would go entirely without my sanction. It is a perfectly impossible thing for a young lady to contemplate. You have never even been on the Continent, and you think of travelling to India unattended."

She had never acted in opposition to her parents, though she had often been domineering to her father in small matters, when he had not resisted. She was always weak, she could only fight when the other side would not fight back. She said, "Oh, father, I must go," and when he said, "Nonsense, I couldn't think of it," she collapsed, partly from cowardice, partly from duty, though her father was not in the least strong-willed either, and with a little serious resistance would have been made to yield. She felt bitterly the reproach in Evelyn's letter, " If only you could have come."

She did not feel as wildly wretched as fifteen years ago, because now in middle age what she passed through at the moment was not of the same desperate importance; but then she had a small corner of hope hidden away that perhaps something might happen, whereas now she realized clearly that the prospect which had given her her chief interest and delight was destroyed for ever.

The trouble told on her, she caught a chill, which developed into pneumonia. She was dangerously ill for some weeks, and when she was better, she was long in getting up her strength, because she had no wish to get well.

Minna and Louie thought it odd that Henrietta should " fret so much about Evelyn's children whom she had never seen. She has always seemed to make so much more fuss over them than over her own nephews and nieces in England. Of course, it was natural that dear Evelyn herself should be distracted, but for Henrietta it almost seemed a little exaggerated."

When she was well enough to travel, the doctor recommended the South of France for the winter, and she went away with a married friend, the Carrie Bostock of the Italian readings.

It was all very pleasant and entertaining to Henrietta, who had never been abroad, never even away from her own family. In the Riviera she could to a certain extent drown thought, but she counted the days with consternation, as each one in its flight brought her nearer to taking up life again at home.

One afternoon she received a letter from her father.

" My dear Henrietta," it ran,

" I do not know if you will be surprised to hear that I am engaged to be married to Mrs. Waters. We have not known one another very long, but I must say I very soon felt that she would be one who could take your dear mother's place. I think it is very possible that you may have observed whither matters were tending. I feel certain that we shall all be very happy together, and I hope you will write her a warm letter of welcome

66

to our family. She will, I am sure, be both mother and sister to you, etc."

The news was staggering to Henrietta. She had been so engrossed in her own trouble that she had observed nothing of what was going on around her. Mrs. Waters, a widow, who had lately settled in the neighbourhood, had been several times to their house and had entertained them at hers, but that she should be anything more than a friendly acquaintance had never entered Henrietta's head. She was to be ousted, her mother was to be ousted, and she was to give a warm welcome to the interloper. Her forgotten temper burst forth. She wrote a violent letter to her father, hurling at him all the ridiculous exaggerated things that most people feel at the beginning of a rage, but which few are so mad as to commit to paper. She refused altogether to write to Mrs. Waters.

She also relieved herself by contradicting everything Carrie said, thus giving her a good excuse for those long talks to a third party, which frequently take place when friends have been abroad together, beginning, " I really had no idea she *could*."

After she had written the letter, as usual she

was very much ashamed. She wrote again unsaying all she had said, but her father had been too much wounded to reply.

She came back just a little before the wedding to see him in quite a new light—a lover, for he at sixty-five and Mrs. Waters at forty-seven had fallen in love.

When Henrietta saw more of her step-mother to be, she had in honesty to own that she liked her. She was not only very attractive, but she was so thoroughly nice and kind, so intent on making people happy, so entirely without airs of patronage, and Henrietta could see how everybody warmed under her smile.

Henrietta had settled that she would not live at home after the marriage. Neither she nor her father could forget the letter, it was better that they should part. She had again asked his forgiveness, but neither felt at ease with the other.

She stayed for a few weeks after Mr. and Mrs. Symons came back from the honeymoon, and saw almost with consternation, how the spirit of the house changed. It became peaceful, cordial, harmonious; it would not have been known for the same house. The whole household liked Mrs. Symons; even her own

dog deserted Henrietta. It was not that she
was ousted from her place, it was that Mrs.
Symons created a place, which never had been
hers. She had had no idea in all these twelve
years how little she had made herself liked.
She had had her chance, her one great chance,
in life, and she had missed it.

When she went away, there were kind good
wishes for her prosperity, interest in her plans,
many hopes that she would visit them, but no
regret ; with a clearness and honesty of sight
she unfortunately possessed she realized that—
no regret.

What was the use of twelve years in which
she had sincerely tried to do her best, if she
had not built up some little memorial of affection ? It was the old complaint of all her life,
" I am not wanted." The anguish she had
shared with Evelyn and her husband had been
much sharper, but in the midst of it there had
been consolation in the exquisite union they
had felt with the children and with one
another. Here there was nothing to cheer
her ; there is not much consolation when one
fails where it seems quite easy for others to
succeed.

Now that it became evident that she would

be so little missed, she was in haste to get the
parting over and be gone. But her unadven-
turous spirit shrank from going out in the
world to manage by itself. She was very
doubtful what she should do. She would not
have been welcomed by Minna or Louie, even
if she had wished to live with them. Her
second brother was in some inacessible foreign
place. Evelyn and Herbert were also far out
of reach. He had exchanged into a regiment
which was quartered at Halifax, in Canada.

But the distance, however great, might have
been faced, if she had not had a miserable
quarrel with Herbert. It began with some
misunderstanding about the tombstone on the
youngest little girl's grave, to which Henrietta
had wished to contribute. She had written to
Evelyn from the Riviera in all the soreness of
worn-out nerves and grief from which the
sublimity has gone. The very fact that they
had been drawn so close to one another made
her specially irritable to Evelyn. After one or
two of her letters, an answer came from
Herbert:

" Evelyn is very ill from all she has been
through, and the doctor says it is most important that she should be kept from every

sort of worry. She was so much distressed at your last letter, and answering you took so much out of her, that I have taken the liberty of keeping this one from her. You have no right to write to her in this way, and I must ask you to drop all correspondence for the present if your letters are to be in the same strain."

Henrietta declared that he was trying to come between her and her sister, and that if that was the case she should never trouble them again. She did not write at all for several weeks, then she felt remorseful, but Herbert could not forgive her. He wrote coldly that Evelyn was still so unhinged as to be incapable of receiving letters without undue excitement.

CHAPTER VII

EVEN now, when there is a certain amount of choice and liberty, a woman who is thrown on her own resources at thirty-nine, with no previous training, and no obvious claims and duties, does not find it very easy to know how to dispose of herself. But a generation ago the problem was far more difficult. Henrietta was well off for a single woman, but she was incapable, and not easy to get on with. She would have thought it derogatory to do any form of teaching—teaching, the natural refuge of a workless woman.

Three or four courses presented themselves. First, philanthropy. She was not really more philanthropic than she had been at twenty, when her aunt had described to her the happiness of living for others. But she felt at nearly forty that charitable work was a reasonable way of filling up her time, on the whole, the most reasonable.

She never had had much to do with poor

people. Mrs. Symons had helped the charwoman, and the gardener, and the driver from the livery-stables, when they were in special difficulties, and Henrietta had continued to do so, and had had her hour at the hospital. That was all. There were the servants, of course, but with the exception of Ellen she looked on servants more as machines made for her convenience, liable to get out of order unless they were constantly watched.

Entirely without enthusiasm, and with a dreary fighting against her lot, she made inquiries among her acquaintances as to where she might find charitable work. At length somebody knew somebody, who knew somebody who was working in London under a clergyman. After further inquiries it was found that the somebody was a lady, who would be very glad if Henrietta would come and live with her, while she saw how she liked the work.

The clergyman, the lady, and all the other workers, were earnest, enthusiastic, high-minded, and full of common sense. Henrietta was not one of these things. She was also very inaccurate, unpunctual, and forgetful, and if her failings were pointed out to her in the gentlest

73

way she took offence, not because she was con-
ceited, but because at her age she was beyond
having things pointed out. She stayed at the
work six months, and during that time she was
always offended with somebody, and sometimes
with everybody.

The work was conducted more on charity
organization lines than was usual in those days;
money was not given without due consideration
and consultation. This was difficult, and required more thinking than Henrietta cared for,
so she saved herself trouble by bestowing five
shillings whenever she wanted, feeling at the
bottom of her heart that if she could not be liked
for herself, she would buy liking rather than not
be liked at all. The five shillings, however, did
not buy either gratitude or affection. She had
always had a grudging way with people of a
different class from herself, and a conviction, in
spite of indiscriminate alms, that she was being
taken in. This infringement of the rules drove
the Vicar to exasperation. His whole heart
was in his work, and Henrietta's disloyalty
hindered him at every turn.

"Can't she be asked to give up meddling in
the parish?" he said to his wife.

"No dear, you know she can't, and she is

very generous, even if she is tiresome. She has often been very helpful to you. You ought to be grateful."

"I'm not grateful," he said, striding about the room; "and then she is so petty, always these absurd squabbles. She hasn't got a spark of love for God or man. That's at the root of it all. We don't want a person of that sort here. If she cared about the people, even if she did pauperize them, I might think her a fool, but I could respect her; but you know she doesn't care for a soul but herself."

"I don't think it is that, but she's in great trouble, I'm sure she is. When you were preaching about sorrow last Sunday, I saw her eyes were filled with tears."

"Were they?" he said, "I'm sorry. But look here, dear, I don't think this sort of work ought to be used as a soothing syrup, or as a rubbish-shoot for loafers, who don't know what else to do. If people aren't doing it because they think it's the greatest privilege in the world to be allowed to do it, I can't see that they do much good."

"I think you're too hard on her."

"Am I? I expect I am. I know I'm fagged to death. She gives Mrs. Wilkins pounds on the sly, which the old lady's been transforming into gin, and then when I explain the circumstances and implore her to leave well alone, she talks my head off with a torrent of incoherent statements, which have nothing whatever to do with the point."

It certainly was true that Henrietta did not do much good, and no one was more aware of this than herself. She stood outside the community, and looked in at them like a hungry beggar at a feast. How she envied their happiness, but she did not feel that she was, or ever could be, a partaker with them. As months passed on, she drew no nearer to them. They were all so busy, so strong in their union with one another, they did not seem to have time to stretch out a friendly hand to one who was at least as much in need of it as Mrs. Wilkins.

The lady she lived with found her trying. "A very trying person" was the phrase that went the round about her, "always criticizing small arrangements about the meals and the housekeeping," for Henrietta could not at first reconcile herself to having no authority to exert, and this jangling was not a good preparation for sisterly sympathy towards her.

The Vicar's wife might have become friends

with her, but during the six months Henrietta was in the parish Mrs. Wharton was ill and hardly able to see anyone. Besides, she was shy, and the only time that Henrietta came to tea they never succeeded in getting beyond a comparison of foreign hotels.

Henrietta would have liked to confide her troubles, but as she grew older she had become a great deal more reserved, and also these troubles she was ashamed to speak of. To think that she had made her own sister, ill and miserable as she was, more ill and more miserable, she could not forgive herself; she was even harder on herself than Herbert had been.

As Mr. Wharton had said, it was useless engaging in this arduous work when her heart was elsewhere. When her six months of trial came to an end, it was clear that the only thing for her was to go. No one could pretend they were sorry, and as everyone imagined she was glad, there seemed no reason to disguise their feelings. They would have been surprised if they had known her thoughts as she sat at the evening service on her last Sunday. "Whatever I do, I fail; what is the use of my living? Why was I born?"

She said to Mr. Wharton in her farewell

interview: "I know I have been very stupid at learning what was to be done, and I have not been willing to take advice. Now I look back, I see the mistakes I have made, and I have done harm instead of good. I want to give you"—she named a large sum considering the size of her income—"to spend as you think right, I hope that may help to make amends. I am very sorry."

He heard a quiver in her voice, and the dislike and irritation he had felt all the six months faded away.

"This is much too generous of you," he stammered. "It is my fault, all my fault. I have been so irritable, I haven't made allowances. My wife tells me of it constantly. I wish you would forgive me and give us another chance. Stay six months longer."

His awkwardness and distress almost disarmed her, but she had felt his snubs, and at nearly forty she was not going to be encouraged like a child. So that though for many reasons she longed to stay, she answered: "Thank you, it was a purely temporary arrangement; I have other plans."

As she walked home she wondered what the other plans were.

When in doubt, go abroad. She went abroad again for three months. Her companion was picked up from nowhere in particular, an odd woman like herself.

They went to Italy. Neither of them cared in the smallest degree for sculpture, architecture, painting, archæology, poetry, history, politics, scenery, languages, or foreigners. These last Henrietta regarded as inferior Anglo-Indians regard natives, referring to them always as "those wretches."

Like most women she loved certain aspects in her garden at home, which were connected with incidents in her life. There was a path bordered by roses, along which they had walked when Evelyn announced her engagement, and a special old apple-tree reminded her of the night her mother died. But to go and admire what Baedeker called a magnificent *coup d'œil* was no sort of pleasure to her.

However, she and Miss Gurney had one unending amusement, which Italy is peculiarly able to supply. They could make short visits to different towns, and fit sights into their days, as one fits pieces into a puzzle. Henrietta found this sport most satisfying.

CHAPTER VIII

JUST as they were getting tired of tables d'hôte
dinners, there came to their hotel an enthusiast
for learning. It was before the days of
women's colleges ; they were established, but
frequented only by pioneers, in whose ranks
no Henriettas are to be found. But courses of
lectures were so ordinary that not even the
most timid could look askance at them. As
philanthropy had failed, and no one could pretend that art could be a resource for Henrietta,
—her career of sketches and two part-songs
had been phenomenally short (invaluable as it
has proved itself for many Englishwomen
suffering from her complaint) — everything
pointed to study as the next solution on the
list.

Study. Henrietta had not read a book
which required any mental exertion since her
dozen chapters of "I Promessi Sposi," fifteen
years ago. Still, the lectures sounded pleasant
to her; they were a novelty, they were—she

could not think of anything else they were—
a novelty must be their claim to distinc-
tion.

She and the travelling friend found a board-
ing-house near the lecture-room. London and
the lodgings both looked dismal after the
brightness of abroad, but they were excited at
the prospect of establishing themselves on their
own account. It was enterprising, but not too
enterprising.

Henrietta found a band of enthusiasts at the
lecture ; it seemed her fate to run up against
enthusiasm she could not share. Young ladies,
middle-aged ladies, even old ladies, all listening
spellbound—at least if not absolutely spellbound,
spellbound compared to Henrietta—to an elderly
gentleman discoursing on Aristotle. For most
of them Aristotle, and the satisfaction of using
their minds were sufficient, but a little knot of
middle-aged women in the front, with hair
inclined to be short, and eyes bursting with
intelligence, used learning as a symbol of
emancipation. Lectures were their vote.
Now they would be in prison.

Henrietta listened for five minutes, then
suddenly her thoughts darted to her port-
manteau: she had lost the key at Dieppe. They

went on to the incivility at the Custom-house,
the incivility of the waiter at Bâle, the incivility
of the gardener at her old home, the geranium
bed in the garden—would her stepmother attend
to it?—her father, was his eyesight really failing?
She came back with a jump to find that the
lecture had moved on several pages. She
listened with fair success for another five
minutes, then her mind wandered to her land-
lady at the lodgings ; was she perfectly honest,
did her expression inspire confidence ? There
was that pearl brooch Louie had given her ;
it was Louie's birthday to-morrow, she must
write, and hear also how Tom was getting on
in this his second term at school, she must send
him a hamper. She had settled the contents
of the hamper when she found that someone
was speaking to her. The lecturer was asking
whether she felt she would care to write a
paper. He hoped as many ladies as possible
would make an attempt at the papers; it would
be a great pleasure and interest to him to look
through them, etc.

On the way back she found Miss Gurney
entranced with everything; she seemed to have
picked up a great deal more than Henrietta.
They went at once to a library and a bookshop

to get what they had been advised to read, and Miss Gurney bought reams of paper. She was hard at work the whole evening. Henrietta had one of the books open before her, but she found the same difficulty in concentrating herself that she had done at the lecture. Miss Gurney was rapidly filling an exercise book with an abstract, and was keeping up a conversation as well.

"Ah *that* was the piece I couldn't quite understand this morning. Yes I see, now it is quite clear. Look, Miss Symons. Oh, I shall learn Greek, I certainly shall, as he said, it will make it twenty times more interesting."

What were they all so excited about? Henrietta had never cared about abstract questions, and she could not see that there was any object in discovering what the ancient Greeks thought about them more than two thousand years ago. The evening before, she and Miss Gurney had had an interesting conversation on the weekly averages of house-books. Then she felt comfortable and on the solid earth. Why then, was she attending lectures on Aristotle? Well, because Miss Gurney had a friend whose cousin had married the lecturer, Professor

Amery, and in the difficult problem of choosing
a subject, when there was nothing she really
cared to know about, this was as good a reason
as any other.

Then Henrietta remembered how she and
Emily Mence years ago at school, had argued
the whole of Saturday afternoon about Mary
Queen of Scots, and had not been on speaking
terms the following day, because Emily had
called Mary frivolous. Had she ever really
been that queer little girl? Still she was
anxious to give the lecturer a chance, most
anxious, for she had already had to suffer from
Minna and Louie's sympathy that the parish
work was a failure. She read three chapters
and fell asleep in the middle of the fourth, and
went to bed half an hour earlier than usual.
Next morning she could not remember a word
of what she had read, but for two dates and
one sentence, which remained in her head.
" Even now, in the latter half of the nineteenth
century, in spite of an unparalleled advance in
our knowledge of the natural sciences, the
world has not yet produced a mind, which can
equal that of Aristotle in its astounding versa-
tility and profundity of learning." She determined to persevere, but was it her subconscious

self which discovered a vast arrear of letters which it was incumbent on her to answer before she thought of anything else?

After the lecture there was a class at which everyone talked. Even the dear old lady next to Henrietta was asking a quavering question. Yes, a little delicate old lady had energy to keep the current of the lecture in her head. She said that Aristotle's problem whether it was possible for slaves to have ordinary virtues, made her think of the difference in the Christian teaching of St. Paul's epistles. Had any of the other Greek philosophers been more humane in their views on slavery? Then another voice struck in, and compared the ancient idea of slavery with the slave code of the United States. The voice was rather strident, but not unpleasant. It had a great deal to say, and for some minutes seemed likely to take the lecture altogether from the mouth of the lecturer. Henrietta looked in its direction, and saw a small apple-cheeked elderly lady. The voice and the face both set her thinking, and by the end of the lecture she was certain that the elderly lady was Miss Arundel. She spoke, and when Miss Arundel had recollected who she was (it took a little time),

Henrietta received a most cordial invitation to tea.

Miss Arundel lived with a niece in a couple of rooms quite close to Henrietta. Mrs. Marston was dead, and Miss Arundel had retired from the school with just enough to live in decent comfort.

" So now, after teaching all my life, I am giving myself the treat of learning, and I can't tell you how I am enjoying it, Miss Symons. Ada and I both like Professor Amery so much." And she prosed on about the lecture and the books she was reading, and did not much care to talk over the old times, which were still very dear to Henrietta. It amazed Henrietta to think that she had once blushed and trembled at the look of this fussy, garrulous little governess.

She might be something of a bore, but there was no question of her happiness, her interest in life. She had been getting up at six the last three mornings that she might finish a book, a large book in two volumes with close print, that had to be returned to the library. Henrietta could imagine nothing in the world for which she would get up at six o'clock. Then her thoughts went like lightning to the morning when the telegram had come telling of little Madeline's death. The wound she had thought healed burst out afresh ; for a few seconds she felt as if she could hardly breathe. Get up at six o'clock, of course she would have forfeited her sleep with joy, night after night. In the midst of envy, she felt something like contempt for Miss Arundel as a child running after shadows.

On her way home, she compared her past with Miss Arundel's. Miss Arundel could look back on busy, successful, happy years. Her room was filled with tributes from old pupils, they were continually writing to her and coming to see her, that Henrietta knew; she did not know how often they had thanked her, and told her what they owed her.

Then she envied Miss Arundel's powers of mind. After forty years of unceasing and exhausting work she seemed as fresh as a schoolgirl, and far more capable of learning, while Henrietta after twenty years of rest, had not merely lost all the qualities she had had as a child, but had gained none from age and experience to take their place. The realization of this fact startled and humiliated her. If her powers had already declined at forty, what was to happen in the twenty years of life that she might reasonably count upon as still before her ?

She thought of Miss Arundel's words : " Etta Symons is a girl with possibilities ; I shall be interested to see how she will turn out." Miss Arundel had long forgotten them, and now looked on Henrietta simply as a co-member of the lectures, but she said to her niece after Henrietta had been to tea, " What a very no-how person Miss Symons is ; I should like to shake her."

Henrietta tried her hardest to work at the lectures, to recover if possible what she had lost, but it was no use. A person of more character and determination might have suc-ceeded, in spite of the long years of mental self-indulgence, so might a person more ready to take advice. But at forty, as I have said, she felt she was beyond advice, so she would not notice Miss Gurney's hints. She chose to despise her numberings and brackets, though she was half-envious of them. And, however contemptible these aids may be to a real student, they were evidently the one hope for Henrietta's foggy mind.

She began a paper on the sly, and with much sweat of brow the following sentence emerged :

"There are a number of celebrated writers in ancient Greece, and among the number we may notice Aristotle, who wrote a number of celebrated books, among which two called the 'Ethics' and 'Republic' are very celebrated. He also wrote many other works, but none are so celebrated as the two above mentioned." She had not written a paper for twenty-three years, and she felt as helpless as if she were trying to express herself in French. Her essays had been well thought of at school.

As she was floundering along, up came Miss Gurney and looked over her shoulder. " Oh Miss Symons, I should have a margin if I were you; I know Professor Amery likes a margin for the corrections, he said so himself. Oh, and you don't mind my saying so, but Aristotle did not write a republic. Shall I just scratch that out ? That was Plato. And I should have a new paragraph there; and I always find, I don't know if you will, that it makes it easier to underline some of the words."

" I am not at all certain that I am going to write a paper," said Henrietta. " I just wrote a few notes down to amuse myself."

" Oh, I'm so sorry, dear. Well, if you should think of doing the paper, you must read this article, it's such a help, it really puts all one wants to say."

"Oh no, I shouldn't care to read that at all."

"Oh do. Let me put it here, and then you can look at it."

"No, thank you."

Miss Gurney went out, and Henrietta sat at her paper for two hours and a half. It was so bad, so unintelligible, that she actually cried over it, and when she heard Miss Gurney's step, she carried it off to her bedroom and locked the door. Miss Gurney was after her in an instant.

"How are you getting on with your paper, dear? Can I be of any help?"

She did finish it at last, and gave it to Mr. Amery. She knew it was bad, but she was too ignorant to know quite how bad. Professor Amery, with the extreme courtesy of elderly gentlemen, wrote: "I think there are one or two points which I have not made quite clear. Would you care to talk them over with me after the class?" But this offer was so alarming that Henrietta "cut" her lectures for two weeks.

There would have been more chance for her, if only she could have become in the least interested. She tried the French Revolution next term for a change, but liked it no better than Aristotle. Intellectual life was dead and buried in her long ago. What would have really suited her best in the present circumstances would have been shorthand and typewriting, but at that time no such occupation was open to her.

She would perhaps have jogged on indefinitely at the lectures, if Miss Gurney, whose great interest was novelty and change, and whose abstracts of learned books had lately become much less voluminous, had not jumped at a suggestion to take a delicate niece abroad, and proposed that Henrietta should come too. So Henrietta consented, and with little regret they gave up the lodgings, and said good-bye to learning.

CHAPTER IX

HENRIETTA paid her father a visit before they started abroad. The promise of the first days was amply fulfilled; the whole house was happy, and Henrietta was touched by the warmth of her welcome. After the squalor of lodgings home was pleasant, and her father's invitation was cordial: "Henrietta, why don't you stay with us? Mildred," with a fond look at his wife, "never will allow your room to be used; it's always ready waiting for you."

It was a temptation to Henrietta, but she refused partly from pride, from a feeling that she ought not to disturb the present comfort, but also because it was getting a principle with her, as apparently with many middle-aged Englishwoman, that she must always be going abroad. Yet she knew that Miss Gurney did not particularly want to have her, and had invited her more from laziness than from anything else.

They went abroad—it was to the Italian Lakes—and a life of sitting in the sun, walking up and down promenades, short drives, and making and unmaking of desultory friendships began. They grumbled a good deal to third parties, but still they were happy enough, according to their low standard of happiness.

As they were abroad for an indefinite period, there was none of the feeling of rush, which they had enjoyed so much before, but sometimes they played the Italian game, and had packed-in days; called, 6.45; coffee, 7.30; train, 8.21; arrive at destination, 11.23; go to Croce d'Oro for coffee, visit churches of Santa Maria and San Giovanni, and museum : *table d'hôte* luncheon, 1.30; drive to Roman remains, back to Croce d'Oro for tea; separate for shopping and meet at station, 5.20, for train, 5.30; back for special *table d'hôte* kept for them in the *salle à manger*. Henrietta would settle it all with Baedeker and the railway guide the night before, and if she had felt apprehension at her failing powers in history, her grasp of this kind of day could not have been bettered. Everything was seen and everything was timed, and the only person who might have something to

93

complain of, was the delicate niece, who went through her treat too exhausted to open her mouth, counting the hours when she might go to her bed in peace.

At last Miss Gurney and the niece decided to return to England. Henrietta found some Americans who wanted to stay at Montreux, and they asked her to join them. After Montreux came Chamounix, and in the autumn Miss Gurney's niece came out again, and she and Henrietta stayed at Como, and then at Mentone till April. Then came Switzerland again. Then Henrietta went to England for a round of visits, and by the end of them she was longing to be back abroad. She said that England was depressing, and gave her rheumatism, and that she (in the best of health and prime of life) could not face an English winter. The fact was she did not care for the sharing of other people's lives which is expected from a visitor, and her long sojourn in hotels with no one but herself to consider, had made her less easy to live with. So without exactly knowing how, she drifted into spending almost all her time abroad. Every other year she came back for visits in the summer, but in the spring, autumn, and winter she wandered from one cheap *pension* to another in Italy, France, Germany, Belgium, or Switzerland.

If she had led a half-occupied life as keeper of her father's house, she now learnt the art of getting through a day in which she did absolutely nothing. When she became accustomed to it, the very smallest service required of her was regarded as a cross. Sometimes a relation would commission her to buy something abroad, and then the *salle à manger* would resound with wails, because she must go round the corner, select an article, and give orders to the shopman to despatch it to England. The friends who asked her to engage rooms for them at an hotel, had cause to rue their request; they never heard the end of it.

Many lonely women receive great solace from their church, and give solace in return. Where would the church and the poor be without them? But Henrietta was never long enough in her caravanserais to become attached to the services of the chaplains in the *salle à manger*, and she soon gave up churchgoing. At first she spent a great deal of time inventing reasons to keep her conscience quiet, such as that it had rained in the night and therefore might rain again, or that she did not approve of

chanting Amen, but later she did not see why
there should be a reason, and left her conscious
to its remorse.

Bad health is another resource for unoccupied
women, and it certainly occurred to her as an
occupation, but she realized that it and roving
cannot be combined, and of the two she preferred roving.

Her chief pastime was to skim through
novels, any novels that could be found, costume
novels of English history by preference. This
was how her bent for learning satisfied itself.
She never remembered the author, or title, or
anything of what she read, but at the same time
she was obsessed with the idea that she must
always have something new, and would constantly accuse her friends, or the library, of
deceiving her with books she had read before.
" If you can't remember, what does it matter ?"
her dreadfully reasonable nieces would exclaim,
not realizing that her sole interest in the novels
was the collector's interest of seeing how many
new ones she could find.

A second pastime was her patience, that
bond which knits together our occidental
civilization. She was always learning new
patiences, and always mixing them up with

one another. This was another source of
annoyance to efficient nieces. "But that is
not demon, Aunt Etta," they would explain,
playing patience severely from a sense of duty.
She cheated so persistently that there was no
room for skill. "I can't conceive why you
play," they said crossly. But the reason was
perfectly clear. It stared one in the face.
During the patience the clock had moved from
ten minutes past eight to twenty-five minutes
to ten.

Henrietta also killed time now and then
with sights ; not churches or old pictures, of
course she never went near masterpieces now
she had ample leisure for seeing them, but
Easter services, royal birthday processions, or
battles of flowers. As she seldom broke her
routine of idleness, these occasions excited her,
not with pleasurable anticipation, but with a
nervous fluster that she might somehow miss
something ; and the concierge, the porter,
Madame, and the head-waiter, would all be
flying about the hotel half an hour before it
was necessary for her to start, sent on some
perfectly useless errand connected with her
outing. If it rained, if something went wrong,
how she grumbled. And when she did see her

show, it gave her very little pleasure. She had not in the least a child's mind; she was not pleased by small events, yet she grasped desperately after them, with an absurd, hazy idea that she was defrauded of her rights, if she did not see them.

Another interest was an enormous collection of photographs of places, which she had not cared for at the time, and could not in the least remember; another her address-book of pensions and hotels, to which she was always adding new volumes; above all, grumbling. Favourite subjects were her kettle and her methylated spirits, whether the hotel would allow her to take up milk and sugar from breakfast, whether the chambermaid abstracted the biscuits she brought from dessert overnight. Everyone who came in contact with Miss Symons found they were made to listen to an endless story of a certain Elise who had stolen the biscuits and substituted other ones that were quite four days old, and of Elise's brazen behaviour when charged with the offence.

Her standard of comfort at a hotel was so impossible that she became an object of terror and dislike to the waiters and chambermaids. She was punctual in payment, but very grasp-

ing, and wrung many concessions from the
hotels by a persistence which no men and few
women would have had the courage to display.
She was always seeking the ideal hotel, and for
this reason she was always wandering, and
never was long enough in one place to strike
any roots and create a feeling of home. This
life corroded her character. She became more
bad-tempered and nagging, always up in arms,
scenting out liberties, and thinking she was
taken advantage of. She was not a character
which does well by itself, and under a domineering manner she concealed her weakness,
vacillation, and timidity. She was divorced
from every duty, every responsibility, every
natural tie, with no outlet for her interest or
her sympathy. It seems inconceivable that
she should willingly have led such an existence.
She was however, much more satisfied with
herself and with things in general, than she had
formerly been. She did not have stormy re-
pentances or outbursts against her lot ; she no
longer desired what was unattainable. If she
did not have a particularly high standard of
happiness or of character, neither, in her
opinion, had the rest of the world. Not that
she thought much of these things. Over-

thinking and over-longing had caused her much misery in early life, and she shrank from opening all those wounds again. She faced facts as little as she could. She lived from day to day, and her inner self was really very much what her outer self seemed, absorbed in the very small round of events which concerned her. The days passed, the months passed, the years passed. She saw them go unregretted, and when they were gone, she did not remember them. Nothing had happened in them, bad or good, to mark their course.

" What a piece of work is a man! How noble in reason, how infinite in faculty, in form, in moving how express and admirable, in action how like an angel, in apprehension how like a god, the beauty of the world, the paragon of animals !"

CHAPTER X

It has been shown that Henrietta had not much power of attracting affection to herself, and she had long ceased to desire it. She was now brought into contact with numbers of different people, and as travelling acquaintances she liked them, but when they parted, she did not want to see them again.

There was, however, an exception to this rule. Henrietta found many companions in misfortune, expatriated either from health, pleasure, or poverty. An intelligent foreigner has inquired whether there are any single elderly ladies left in England, so innumerable are the hosts abroad. Some, like her, had worn their personalities so thin that it seemed likely they would eventually become shadows with no character left; others were nice and cheerful, and made little encampments in the wilderness, so that the unfortunates might gather round them, and almost feel they had got a home.

It was in the room of a nice one that Henrietta met a Colonel. There are fewer occupationless Englishmen abroad, but there is a fair supply—half-pay officers, consumptives, and mysterious creatures, who have no good reason for being there. They were a strange medley for Henrietta to associate with, people whom in her palmy days, as mistress of her father's house, she would have thought unspeakable. She had none of this generation's tolerance and love of new sensations to attract her to unsatisfactory people. She only really liked conventional respectability.

This Colonel was not respectable. He was not a Colonel in the English army, and never would say much about himself. He was very pleasant and polite, and Henrietta, as she walked back to table d'hôte, felt she had spent a livelier afternoon than usual. It was at the beginning of the season, and looking back six weeks later she was astonished to find how often they had met.

Shortly after, the lady in whose room Henrietta had first seen him, asked her to tea. She did not seem quite so easy-going as usual, and at last began: "You know, Miss Symons, my cousin, Colonel Hilton, is rather a peculiar

man. I've known him all my life, and I
don't think there is any harm in him, but
money is his difficulty. He ought to be well
off, but it always seems to slip through his
fingers."

Henrietta realized that this was a warning.

At the end of the season he proposed and
she accepted him. She knew he proposed for
her money, and she knew that, besides being
mercenary, he was a poor creature in every
way. Most people could not have borne long
with his society, but she, unaccustomed to
companionship, felt that he sufficed her. She
did not think much of the future. When she
did, she realized that it was hardly possible
they could marry. But meanwhile it was
something—she would have been ashamed to
own how much—to have someone call her
" dear." Once he attained to " dearest," but
he was evidently frightened at his temerity, and
did not repeat the experiment.

She announced the engagement, and a letter
from Minna came flying to the Riviera, saying
that all sorts of terrible things were known
about the Colonel, and imploring Henrietta to
desist. She did not desist, but very soon the
Colonel did, having discovered that her fortune

was not so large as he had been given to
suppose. There was a solid something it is
true, but for Henrietta, quite middle-aged and
decidedly cross (she imagined she was never
cross with him), he felt he must have a very
considerable something. He wrote a letter
breaking off the engagement, and left the
Riviera abruptly, having made a good thing out
of his season. Henrietta had lent him, *he*
said—given, others said—over three hundred
pounds.

"And now we shall have a terrible piece of
work," said Minna to Louie. "You know what
Henrietta always is—what she was about that
other affair with a man years ago, and again
when Evelyn's little girl died. She gets so
excited and overwrought."

But Henrietta quite upset their expectations.
This, which most people might have thought
the most serious misfortune which had befallen
her, affected her very little. In her heart of
hearts she was saying : "Well, when all's said
and done, I've had my offer like everyone else."
She was grateful for the "dears" too. She
did not realize that there had been absolutely
nothing behind them. She answered the
Colonel's speedy application for more money,

and continued to send him supplies from time to time.

Evelyn and Herbert had returned to England, and had settled on the South Coast. Two boys had been born in Canada, and had grown and prospered. Henrietta stayed with Evelyn for a fortnight whenever she was back in England, but somehow the visits were not the pleasure they should have been.

Evelyn was still delicate, and Herbert had begged Henrietta when she saw her, to make no allusion to their loss. Evelyn was delighted at showing her boys, and Henrietta was pleased for her that she should have them, but to her they did not in the least take the place of the dead. They were not hers; she was almost indignant with Evelyn for caring for them so much, and accused her in her heart of forgetfulness. This made her irritable, which Herbert resented, and then Evelyn was nervous because Herbert and Henrietta did not get on well together. Evelyn's letters to her were very affectionate, the only real pleasure, in any reasonable sense of the word, in Henrietta's life.

Sometimes Evelyn and her husband and boys came out to stay with Henrietta. The visits were not occasions of much happiness, and a certain day remained for years as a mild nightmare in Evelyn's memory. They were all in Milan one spring, when the patron of the hotel announced that his lady cousin, who lived at some out-of-the-way little country town, had heard from her friend, a priest in that same little town, that on Tuesday there was to be a special festa in connection with a local saint. Would the English ladies and gentlemen care to go? The patron himself had the contempt of an enlightened man for saints and festas, but he knew the curious attraction which such childishness possesses for the English tourist.

All was arranged. The railway company had never intended that the little town should be reached from Milan, but with an early start and much changing of trains it was possible to accomplish the journey in two hours and a half.

They arrived. There was no surprise among the hotel omnibuses at their appearance, for the Italians have found that the English will turn up everywhere; but to-day they were certainly the only representatives of their nation.

They reached the church where the festa was to take place. It was sleeping peacefully, brooded over by a delicious, sweet smell of dirt and stale incense.   Not a soul was to be seen. But as the party marched indignantly up and down the aisles, another smell comes to join the incense—garlic. A merry, good-humoured little priest appears ; it is the friend of the lady cousin.

He knew no English but " Yis, Yis"; they little Italian but the essentials for travel: "Troppo, bello, antiquo." At the word "festa" he shook his head very sadly, and he said " Domani " so many times that, with the help of Henrietta's little phrase-book, they found it must mean " To-morrow." They had come the wrong day. He was very much distressed about it.   To make up, if possible, for the disappointment, he showed them all over the church and sacristy ; he did not miss one memorial tablet, not one disappearing fresco, and knowing the taste of the English, he said, as each new item was displayed : " Molto, *molto* antiquo."

He was so much attracted by Evelyn's charming middle-aged beauty and her sweet English voice that when Santa Barbara's was exhausted, he could not resist showing them, what he cared for much more, his own little brand-new mission church, with its brilliant rosy-cheeked images and artificial wreaths. The boys, fifteen and seventeen, had had enough of churches after two days at Milan, and Evelyn could hear from Herbert's conscientious, stumping tread that he was examining the church because a soldier must always do his duty.

At length it was over; they came out into the sunshine, and the big town clock struck a quarter to eleven. Their train home left at 5.30. The two churches had only used up an hour and a quarter.

"Now, dearest," said Herbert firmly, "I dare say you and Etta will like a little rest. Suppose I and the boys get a walk in the country; and don't wait lunch for us, you know. I dare say we can get something at one of those little wine places one sees about."

They managed to construct a sentence for the priest, who was standing nodding by them: "Are there any pretty walks in the neighbourhood?"

Smiling genially, he pointed to an answer which the phrase-book translated: "The landscape presents a grandiose panorama."

Evelyn gave the priest a contribution to his mission church. He was overwhelmed with surprise and pleasure at this good action on the part of a heretic, it added to his pleasure that she was such a beautiful heretic, and when, as they said good-bye, Evelyn wished that they might meet again, he replied, with his face all over smiles, "I hope perhaps in Paradise"; he could not speak with absolute certainty. Something in the way he said it brought tears to Evelyn's eyes, and Henrietta, who was looking on and listening, thought with a little envy that none of the many priests or pastors, few even of the laity she had encountered in her wanderings, had ever hoped to meet *her* again either in heaven or on earth. After many affectionate bows, he said good-bye.

The sisters were scarcely half an hour buying picture postcards (there had been nothing else to do, so they had bought more picture postcards than it seemed possible could be bought), when rain came on—not gentle English rain, but the fierce cataracts of Italy, let loose for the rest of the day. Back came Herbert and the boys, who had somehow missed the grandiose panorama. It had, in fact, been created entirely out of politeness by the priest.

After lunch, which they prolonged to its farthest limit, there was nothing for it but the salon, a small room, with its window darkened by the verandah outside. Madame brought in yesterday's *Tribuna*, and they found an illustrated catalogue of hotels in Dresden. Oh, that three hours and a half ! The boys and Herbert would have been content to sit with their shoulders hutched up, staring at their boots, going every quarter of an hour to the front-door to see if it were raining as hard there as it was out of the salon window, and Evelyn only wanted to be left in silence with her headache. But Henrietta would tease the boys. Whatever they did do, or whatever they did not do, seemed an occasion for criticism. Evelyn, to divert attention, burst into long reminiscences of the days at Willstead. Henrietta combated each statement with a kind of sneer, as though whatever Evelyn said was bound to be worthless. Evelyn saw Herbert, who always treated her as if she were a wonderful queen, casting black looks at Henrietta. At last his anger came out :

" I don't know why it seems impossible for you to talk to Evelyn with ordinary civility, Henrietta."

" My dearest boy," said Evelyn, going and patting Herbert's shoulder, " Etty and I don't care about ordinary civility. We love having our little spars together. Sisters don't bother to be as polite as men are to one another; life would be much too much of a burden!"

She gave Henrietta's hand a squeeze, as she went back to her seat, but after this Henrietta would hardly talk at all, and the reminiscences became a monologue from Evelyn.

At last, at long last, the train came, and Henrietta forgot her disappointment in sleep. The happy day she had looked forward to, and planned, and paid for, was over.

Louie and her Colonel did not thrive better as the years went on. Money never seemed able to stay with them. Henrietta helped them long after everyone else had become tired of them. She did not expect gratitude, nor did she get it. In spite of her dependence, Louie managed to convey the impression of Henrietta's inferiority, and the children spoke of her as a butt.

"Oh, it's Aunt Etta's year; it really is rather a fag to think we shall have her for three weeks. Ethel, it's your turn to take her in tow; I had her all last time."

"Poor Etta!" said Minna; "she is such an interminable talker, it does worry Arthur so. She means very well; we all know that."

Minna's children were very much of the

twentieth century, and were not going to bear with a dull old maid, merely because she was their aunt and had been kind to them. As one of them expressed it, "Never put yourself out for a relation, however distant. That's an axiom."

Little as the younger generation thought of her, she thought something of them, and the second week in December, when she chose her Christmas presents for all her nieces and nephews, was the pleasantest week in the year to her.

CHAPTER XI

HENRIETTA had been fourteen years abroad, when she came to pay her biennial visit to Evelyn.

"Who do you think has come to live here, Henrietta?" said Evelyn, as they sat talking the first evening. "Ellen."

"Ellen?"

"Yes, our dear old Ellen—Mrs. Plumtree. She's a widow now. Her eldest son is working here, and she is living with him and his wife. I went to see her last week, and she was so delighted to talk over old times, and when she heard you were coming, she was so excited. You were always her favourite."

A few days afterwards they went, to find Ellen a very hale old lady. In spite of having brought up a large family of her own, she had the clearest remembrance of apparently every incident of the childhood of "you two young ladies" (so she still called them) as though she had never had any other interest in life.

" Oh, and, Miss Etta," she said, " what a
sight you did think of Miss Evie ! I never knew
a child take so to anyone before. ' She's quite
a little mother,' I often used to say to Sarah.
Do you remember Sarah ? She died only last
year ; she suffered dreadful with her heart. Do
you remember how you always would go to
put your hand into the water before I gave
Miss Evie her bath, because you wanted to be
sure it wasn't too hot ? Every evening you
did it ; and one day you were out late, and
Miss Evie was in bed before you came in,
and you cried because you hadn't been able to
do it."

Neither sister found it easy to speak, but
Ellen wanted very little encouragement.

" Sometimes as a great treat, when you was a
little older, Miss Evie, I let you sleep in Miss
Etty's bed, and she used to lay and cuddle you
so pretty. And the canary, Miss Etta—do
you remember that ? When Miss Evie's dickie
died, you went all the way to Willstead by
yourself and bought a new canary, so that she
might never know her dickie died. Your
mamma was very angry with you, I remember ;
but there was nothing you wouldn't do for
Miss Evie."

The sisters walked back in silence; their hearts were too full for speech. There was no time for private conversation till night, when Evelyn came into Henrietta's room, and flung her arms round her.

"Darling, darling Etta," she said, "I could hardly bear it, when Ellen was talking. To think of all that you were to me, all that you did for me, and that I should have forgotten it. Oh, how is it that we've got apart?"

"I don't know," said Henrietta; "I don't think there is anything much to like in me. No one does care for me. I think if no one likes one, one doesn't deserve to be liked."

"Oh, nothing in this life goes by deserts."

"People love you, and they're quite right; you ought to be loved. You did care for me once, though. Herbert wrote — you know, when we lost—'A good cry with you will be more comfort to Evelyn than anything else.' Even then, in the middle of it all, it made me happy."

"Oh, Etta, what you were to me then!"

Henrietta took Evelyn's hand and squeezed it convulsively. When she could speak, she said: "Evelyn, do you ever think of our children?"

"Think of them—of course I do. Do you, Etta?"

"I used to, but I tried not to—it was too bitter. The children were what I lived for, and I don't think of them often now. It's past and gone."

"Oh, I couldn't live if I didn't. I don't think it is bitter now. These dear boys, they're not quite the same to me as the ones that were taken."

"I thought you'd forgotten them."

"I thought you had, Etta, and I couldn't help feeling it."

"Herbert asked me never to speak about them to you."

"Dear Herbert, he is so good—I can't tell you how good he is to me—but he never will mention them. First of all I was so ill, I couldn't stand talking of them, but now I can, and I do long for it. He doesn't forget them, I know, but I think men live more in the present than we do; and he has his work, which absorbs him very much, and it isn't quite the same for a man. And then they were so delicate, particularly Madeline, that I was wrapped up in them all their lives; and they were so small, he couldn't see much of them."

" Do you feel that you could tell me about them ?"

" Yes, I should like to."

They talked far into the night. Herbert was away, so that there was no one to stop them, and when at last the dawn drove them to bed, Evelyn said : " I can't tell you how much good you've done me. I seem to have been living for this for fifteen years."

They neither of them slept at all that night. Both were full of remorse, but Henrietta's was the bitterest. The life which had seemed to do quite well enough all these years, suddenly appeared to her as it was. She contrasted her present self with the little girl Ellen had known. Like Jane Eyre, she " drew her own picture faithfully without softening one defect. She omitted no hard line, smoothed away no displeasing irregularity." She had squabbled, that very afternoon, if it is possible to squabble when only one party does the squabbling, all the way down to Ellen's about various quite unimportant dates in William's life. The incident was almost as much a part of her day's routine as eating her breakfast. Now it seemed to her a manifestation of the degradation into which she had fallen.

The power and vividness of her memory, magnified ten times by the mysterious agency of midnight, brought back the words of advice of Emily Mence, of Minna, and of her aunt, just as if they had been spoken last week. She had entirely forgotten them for years. Now they kept rushing through her head hour after hour.

Before breakfast Evelyn came into her room, her eyes shining with agitation, and looking so flushed that Henrietta saw what need there had been for Herbert's caution.

" Etty," she said, " I've been thinking all night ; I can't bear your living in this horrible way : no home, away by yourself, so that we see nothing of you. Come and live here, live with us. We shan't interfere with you ; you shall come and go as you like. Or live in the village, there is a dear little house just made for you. Only come and be near us."

Henrietta was sorely tempted, it was a great sacrifice to say no. But she knew that Herbert only tolerated her for Evelyn's sake, and that the boys, rather spoilt and self-important, found her a nuisance. She knew also that she could not trust herself to be pleasant and good-tempered. If she came, it would not be for Evelyn's happiness. So she refused, and even in her fervour of love for Henrietta, Evelyn could not help realizing it was best that she should.

At the same time that talk was a turning-point in Henrietta's life. She never felt after it that she was completely unwanted. Although she would not live with Evelyn, she thought she might justifiably come and be much nearer her, and she gave up the roving life and returned to England. It had in fact satisfied her, only because she had felt so uncared-for that she became insignificant even to herself.

Where should she live? She knew that every place where she had relations would not do, but this only ruled out four of the towns of the United Kingdom. It must be a town; on that point she was clear. As she cared for none of the special advantages of a town, its more lively society, its greater opportunities for entertainment and intellectual interests, she was particularly insistent that she could not do without them. What she wanted was a house with room for herself, two maids, and a couple of visitors. Such a house is to be found in tens and hundreds everywhere. She went round and round England in a fruitless search.

As a *pension habituée* the whole arrangement of her life had been taken out of her hands ; even her clothes had been settled for her by one of those octopus London firms which like to reduce their customers to dummies; and her transit from hotel to hotel, and from English visits back to hotels, had become a mere automatic process. She had not made a decision for so many years that though her nieces and nephews were witty over her vacillation, and declared that she enjoyed being a nuisance, it was a fact that she was trying her best to be sensible and competent. She, with no go-between, no protector, must determine which was most important— gravel soil or southern aspect. She felt as she had felt years ago, when she wrote her paper for Professor Amery, only ten times more bewildered, almost delirious.

Of course, her nieces constantly talked her over, shaking their heads and saying : " If only Aunt Etta would let us." But however weak she was, she was firm in this : she would *not* be helped. The outward sign of her bewilderment was extreme crossness, particularly to Evelyn, who was allowed to accompany her in her search, and to hear her remarks without making any suggestions. " I will thank you to let me decide about my own house by myself." They had examined nine houses that day, and were both almost weeping with exhaustion.

Evelyn could not help feeling exasperated, but when Etta stumbled the moment after from sheer nervousness, and Evelyn caught hold of her hand, she realized from its hot trembling grasp how hard it is to come back to life again.

Henrietta would probably never have found the right spot, if a timely attack of rheumatism had not persuaded her to fix on Bath. When she had settled into her house at last, she hated it. She dismissed five servants in two months. She was so dull, no one called; Bath was so cold. If only she could let her house and go abroad for the winter. Happily no suitable tenant appeared, and gradually Bath grew into a habit and she became resigned. But it was long, very long, before she would own that she liked it.

CHAPTER XII

AND now a happier and more useful course of life began. Henrietta had just enough rheumatism to take a course of waters sometimes. She found a doctor who had a great *flair* for elderly ladies; he knew when to bully them, when to flatter them, and when to neglect them. He and the waters made a centre round which the rest of her interests might group themselves. Church. She found a vicar with nothing of Mr. Wharton's enthusiasm and loftiness of aim, but with a greater realization of people's capacities. He too had made a study of elderly ladies, who are always such an important branch of congregations. He could see that what Miss Symons was in his drawing-room, touchy, incompetent, and snappish she would be in any work she did in the parish. But he was also made to see her extreme generosity, of which she herself was entirely unconscious. He liked and was touched by her humility. " Oh no, don't trouble about asking me, Mr. Vaughan, nobody will want to talk to a dull person like me. Get some nice young men for the girls, if you can." "No, I can't have that pretty Miss Allan helping at my stall, I can get along very well by myself. I shall bring Annie; we can manage together."

The poor people, of course, did not like her, for as she grew older she was more convinced than ever that the lower orders must be constantly reproved. But poor people are very magnanimous, and they were sure of a good many presents. She was also for ever bickering with her servants, but "poor old lady" as they said, "she's getting on now, it makes her worry," and she found in Annie one who knew how to give at least as good as she got. Horror of being defrauded by servants and tradespeople was a great resource, and though she continually deplored the pleasure of life abroad, these years of muddling in and out of her house, her garden, and her shops, were probably the happiest in her life.

A certain conversation contributed not a little to this new happiness. She was at a tea-party, for once she had been admitted into the circle of tea-parties, she became much absorbed in them, and she and a neighbour were tracing an attack of influenza from its source to its decline, when Henrietta's hostess came up to her.

"I want to introduce you to Mrs. Manson," said she. "Mrs. Manson is a cousin of that Mr. Dockerell you told me you knew, Miss Symons."

There had been no sentiment in Henrietta's telling, she had quoted Mr. Dockerell as an authority on Portugal laurels.

"Ah, my cousin, Mr. Dockerell," said Mrs. Manson, "you knew him, did you? He's dead, poor man, had you heard? He died last year."

And once started upon Mr. Dockerell, she rambled away with his life's history, being one without much feeling, who could say everything to anybody.

"Poor Fred, his marriage was such a mistake. She was older than him, and a mass of nerves. She caught him. I always said it was that; anybody on earth could have caught him. It was at Worthing; those seaside places in the summer are very dangerous. My mother used to say: 'We must be thankful it isn't worse.' No, he wasn't happy. There was a story that

124

he really liked somebody else: a Miss Simon
her name was—Simon, or something like that.
Where did she come from? Oh yes, Willstead; he had some work there at one time.
' The beautiful dark Miss Simon.' At least, she
wasn't beautiful, that was our joke; there was
a pretty sister, but she was fair. My sister
always insisted he was pining after her, but
that wasn't like Fred. We used to be hard-
hearted, and declare it was indigestion."

Mr. Dockerell's death was not very much to
Henrietta, he had passed so entirely out of her
life. But "a dark Miss Simon living at Willstead, not beautiful "; she thought much of that.
She could not but believe it must be herself.
"So perhaps after all he did care," she said to
herself, as she sat over the fire that evening,
she had reached the age when she liked a good
deal of twilight thinking undisturbed by the
gas. But the news had come so late; if only
she had known before. Those months and
years of unhappiness rose before her. Granted
that Providence had decreed they were not to
marry, and looking back she did not feel as if
she wished they had married, it was all so far
behind her, she thought that she might have
been given the happiness of a farewell letter

from him, telling her that she really was first in his heart. "I should never have seen him or heard from him again; of course I should not have wanted it, but it would have been so comfortable to have known." She fell into her childhood's habit of daydreams, if one can have daydreams of the past, and sat such a long time absorbed that Annie came in at last with her matchbox. "Don't you want the gas lit, 'm? You never rang, I was gettin' quite fidgettin' about you, your heart's not very strong."

Henrietta was composing his last letter, each moment making it more and more tender. She came back with a start to ordinary life, and the magazine article on "Beauties of George II.'s Court," which lay open before her. She dismissed her picture of what might have been with "Of course it was impossible, it's ridiculous wondering about it. How can one be so foolish at nearly sixty?" But she did wonder, and there is no doubt she was very much pleased. And after all the good news was false, he had never thought of her again.

She confided the little incident to Evelyn. Evelyn, adoring her husband and adored by him, had been so much accustomed to men's admiration that she did not attach great value to it. She had seen long ago her old lovers pairing happily with somebody else: that side of life had been over for herself many years since. Her interest now was in her sons' possible marriages, and it was a little painful to her that Henrietta should be so much excited about what had never after all been more than a potential love affair. To tell the truth, she thought it a trifle petty and not worthy the dignity of one on the verge of old age. She wanted to be sympathetic, and she was too kind to say anything that would wound, but Henrietta could see that Evelyn did not enter into her feelings.

Louie's children were now started in life, and the sons were getting on so well that even Henrietta owned they might be expected to take the burden of their parents upon themselves. She had her nieces and nephews to stay; Minna and Louie also came to take the waters. One or two of the nieces were of course collecting second-hand furniture, and used Bath as a centre for expeditions to the little country towns. The visits were very pleasant, if they did not last more than two nights; after two nights there would be a

127

danger of friction, and sometimes friction itself. Her nieces and nephews were all what she called "modern," the harshest word but one she knew. A certain nephew and niece, alas, were more than modern—they were the harshest word of all, "*Radical*." The nephew had too profound a contempt for old ladies to talk about anything more controversial than the local train service, but even that he discovered was a topic beyond Henrietta's capacity. For it turned out, after she had appeared to be talking very sensibly about the afternoon trains, that she was referring to one marked with an "N.," a Thursday excursion, which destroyed all the point of her remarks. Her nephew explained this to her, but she would stick to her train, and declare that the "N." was a misprint. A misprint in Bradshaw. What a mind! He had not realized that even an aunt could be so childish. Of course she knew she was wrong, but she tried to persuade herself that she was right, because she was so much disappointed. She had wanted to make a good impression on her nephew, even if he were a Radical. She thought men superior to women, though throughout her life her affection and veneration had been given to women—Miranda,

Miss Arundel, Evelyn. She had an innocent conviction that men knew more about everything, except perhaps the youngest babies, and she was anxious for masculine good opinion. Alas, to contradict her nephew several times running was not the way to win him over.

He felt that contradiction amply justified him in wrapping himself up in his paper for the rest of the evening, vouchsafing "um" and "ah" occasionally after imploring pressure from his aunt. He left first thing next morning.

Then his Radical sister came. She inspected something under Government, and with a burning faith in womanhood hoped against hope that with time her aunt must be converted "to think the right things." With a mere niece Henrietta felt at liberty, and very competent, to correct. But she little knew with whom she was reckoning.

"Servants belong to a Trade Union, Annie and Emma" (the cook) "join a Union. How perfectly ridiculous!"

"But why ridiculous, Aunt Etta?"

"Because it is."

"No, but do tell me, Aunt Etta. I know

there must be some solid reason, and I should
be so much interested to hear it."

"You should have seen Annie's hat last
Sunday : enormous pink roses in it."

"Yes," answered her niece, catching her aunt
out very easily, "but as far as that goes some
ladies have enormous pink roses."

"Yes, indeed.   Why, when I was young we
should never——"

"And you don't object to their joining Trade
Unions ?"

"Yes, I do."

"But, after all, what is that Teachers' Society
that Hilda belongs to" (Hilda was another
niece) "but a Trade Union ? And you went on
their excursion, Hilda told me."

"That has nothing to do with it " (a favourite refuge with old ladies when they are getting
the worst of a discussion).   "Of course, if
Hilda——"

"So I mean Annie's wearing garish hats is
not really a reason against her joining a Trade
Union.   You see my point, don't you ?"

"I particularly dislike being interrupted.   I
hadn't finished what I was going to say."

"I beg your pardon, Aunt Etta, I am so
sorry.   What was it you were going to say ?"

Henrietta could not remember, and branched off to something else. "Wearing all this jewellery in the day is so common. That girl at the post office had two brooches and a locket, and she kept me waiting so long; she always does."

"Yes, but I think we must leave them to judge what they like to wear; it is not our business really, is it? But I did just want to speak to you about this Servants' Union, Aunt Etta. I wonder if I might give Annie a little pamphlet I have written about it. Of course, we don't want them to be always striking or anything of that sort. The aim of my Society is simply to try and rouse servants to a sense of what it is they're missing—this great power of organization and solidarity which they ought to have. I think Annie looks such a nice intelligent girl, who would be sure to have an influence with her friends."

"No, she's most tiresome and inconsiderate. She *would* go out this evening just when you were coming, because she wanted to take her mother to the hospital, so that I had to have Mrs. Spring, and it is all very well for Annie to say——"

"I wonder if I might read you a little piece

out of my pamphlet, Aunt Etta, just to make a few points clear. You see, I want to get you in favour of our Union so much, because we feel that mistresses ought to be co-operating with the servants, helping them to help themselves, and then we shall get a really influential body of public opinion, which will do valuable work in improving servants' conditions."

Henrietta writhed and struggled, and went off on frivolous pretexts, but she could not escape the pamphlet, which was extremely able ; so was the author extremely able, but for a complete ignorance of human nature. Henrietta heard all about Socialism, Land Taxes, and Adult Suffrage too, and the more cross she became the more kindly and patiently Agatha shouted, greeting any specially absurd ebullition with imperturbable pleasantness, and "how interesting, I am *so* anxious to get exactly at your point of view." That niece was not invited again.

Henrietta often thought with affection and gratitude of the little old aunt, who had died many years back ; but, as she would have been the first to own, her old age was not nearly so successful. Her house was not a centre for everybody. She had some elderly ladies

with whom she exchanged visits, but young
people disliked her, and children were afraid
of her.

Ever since she settled in England, she had
made earnest attempts to curb her temper.
But the companion of a lifetime is not easily
shaken off at fifty-five, and more often than
not she was quite unaware of crossness, from
which all around were suffering severely. On
the very rare occasions that she did realize it,
she went back to the self she had been as a
child, descended from the pedestal of her age
and generation, and said she was sorry.

One day she and Annie had a long serious
battle. The question in the first instance was
whether Annie had chipped off the nose of the
china pug-dog on the mantelpiece, a relic of
the old house at Willstead; Henrietta always
had a tender feeling for relics. The arguments marshalled by Annie were against
Henrietta, but arguments never had much
weight with her. Besides, the battle passed on
from the definite point of the nose to vague
but bitter attacks on character. Henrietta
always had in her mind an ideal servant, who
accepted scolding not merely with meekness
but with gratitude, and was fond of quoting

her, to the exasperation of the real servants. After half an hour Annie began to cry noisily, so that Henrietta's words were drowned. The interview came to an end. Annie went downstairs and told Cook, but she wasted few tears or thoughts on the matter, and almost at once they were laughing cheerfully over their young men, as they sat at needle-work.

Henrietta did think, fidgeting about the room while she thought, taking things out of their places and putting them where they ought not to be, in a fuss of discomfort. At last she rang the bell.

" The lamp, please, Annie."

" The lamp 'm," said Annie; " but you don't want it for half an hour yet, do you, 'm, it's such a beautiful evening ?"

It was impossible ever to quell Annie.

" The lamp, please," repeated Henrietta, " and I should like to—I think you ought to —I feel that in a—what I want you to realize is that you should keep a great watch over your temper. When one comes to my age one sees that there is—and you should not put it off till too late as people sometimes—as I have done."

Annie's sharp ears heard the last little murmur. Henrietta rather hoped they would not, though it was for the sake of the murmur that she had rung the bell.

Annie said "Yes 'm," very pleasantly, and yielded about the lamp. She told cook afterwards, with some amusement, "She's funny, I've always said that, but," she added, "I've known some I should say was funnier."

This opinion may be worth recording, as it was one of the highest tributes to her character Henrietta ever received.

On the whole during those latter years she improved, and in the general reformation of her character she raised the standard of her reading. She confined herself in the mornings and afternoon to mildly scandalous memoirs of Frenchwomen and biographies of Church dignitaries, keeping her costume novels for the evening.

She often saw Evelyn, and they talked of the past, but they never regained the almost heavenly intimacy of that night. They seldom met without some disagreeableness from Henrietta, and she did not like the boys, there was nothing of Evelyn in them, while they for their part could not imagine why their mother cared for their aunt Henrietta. It was a continual struggle for Evelyn not to be impatient with her; much as she longed to, she could not keep on the high plane of devotion, which had brought such happiness to both.

CHAPTER XIII

HENRIETTA died when she was sixty-three. Her father and stepmother were long dead, also her second brother, whom none of the family had seen for years. When her relations were sent for, it was very cold weather in January, and Louie and Minna did not obey the summons. They deplored it continually afterwards, and explained to one another how appalling the wind had been, and what care they had to take for their children's sake, and how Henrietta had frightened them so much the year before by sending for them when there was no need, that they naturally could not be expected to realize that this time it really was important.

William came, looking more benevolent than ever with his very becoming white hair. Henrietta said that she thought it was the last time she should see him, but he assured her it was just the cold which had pulled her down a little, and she would be all right again as soon as the

wind changed. " It's wretched, knocks everybody up." He looked so hearty and mundane
that it almost seemed, when he was in the room,
as if there could not be such a thing as death.

They talked about the drought last summer,
and William's son, who was a planter in Ceylon,
and the noise of the motor-buses in London,
until William said he must go for his train.
He was allowing a quarter of an hour too
much time, for he was able to stay and talk a
little while with the doctor, who called when
he was there.

"There isn't any chance, you say."

"No, I am afraid not. Miss Symons' heart
has been delicate for some years ; it gives her
very little strength to stand against this attack."

"Um! I was afraid so," said William, and he
was glad to get out of the house, and buy a
Pall Mall.

The inspector niece came down (uninvited),
very energetic, and very kind in using the last few
days of her holidays in nursing a disagreeable
reactionary relation. She dominated the nurse,
who was much meeker than nurses usually are,
and quite quelled her poor aunt, too weak to
protest even at attacks on the monarchy. But
Henrietta was much happier when the niece's

holidays came to an end, and she was left to die quietly and dully with the nurse.

Evelyn was away in Egypt with Herbert for her health, and by a most unfortunate accident she did not get the first telegram announcing Henrietta's dangerous illness. Poor Henrietta asked constantly if there was nothing from her, and as she got weaker, and a little wandering, she kept on crying like a child: "I want Evelyn." They cabled again, and when the answer came, "Starting home at once," it was too late, and Henrietta was not sufficiently herself to understand it.

As soon as Evelyn got home, she went to Bath. The little house was still as it was, but for some legacies which a careful nephew had already abstracted. But the place of the dead seemed to have been filled even more quickly than usual. Annie, as she said, had only waited "till the pore old lady was taken" to marry comfortably with a saddler, and the parlourmaid was already established in a very smart town situation. There was an unknown caretaker to look after the house, which was to let. Evelyn saw the doctor and the clergyman, who both spoke kindly of Miss Symons. "We shall miss your sister very much," said Mr.

Vaughan, " she was always doing kind things,"
—and he did miss her to a certain extent, but
there is a ceaseless supply of generous, touchy
incapable old ladies in England, and he could
not be expected to miss her very much.
Evelyn went to see the nurse, and could hear
from her more of what she wanted. The
nurse was a kind, sweet girl, the centre of an
affectionate family, and engaged to a devoted
young clerk.

"Oh, Mrs. Ferrers, if only you could have
come back in time," she said, sobbing, " or if
you could have written. She *did* want you so ;
every time there was a ring it was, ' Is that
from her ?' and I heard her say to herself : ' I
thought she would be *sure* to come.' I simply
had to go out in the passage, I couldn't keep
back my tears, and of course one must always be
bright before a patient ; it is so bad for them if
one isn't. Some nieces and nephews came,
and one of them stayed several days, and two
brothers, I think ; and there were several
members of the family there for the funeral,
and she had some simply lovely wreaths, and
the church was nice and full, numbers of her
poor people were there," brought there, as
surely the kind nurse knew, not from love of

Henrietta, but from love of funerals, "but when your wire did come I cried for joy, though we couldn't make her take it in, poor dear; still it seemed as if someone really cared for her. Oh, she looked so lovely and peaceful at the end, all the trouble gone."

This was a comforting deception, which the nurse thought it justifiable to practise on relations, for in fact death had not changed Henrietta; there had been no transfiguration to beauty and nobility, she looked what she had been in life—insignificant, feeble, and unhappy.

"Miss Symons asked me to give you this box," said the nurse. "She made me promise I would give it you over and over again."

Evelyn found it was an inlaid sandalwood box, which she had sent from India as a present from the first baby. In it she found Herbert's letter announcing the death of little Madeline, hers and the other two babies' photographs, and a sheet of notepaper, tied with blue ribbon. On it was written, "I can't tell you how much good you have done me, I seem to have been living for this for fifteen years. EVELYN, September 23, 1890." As she read it, Evelyn remembered, what she had long forgotten, that this was what she had once said to Henrietta.

When she walked to the hotel, it was a bright, sunny afternoon, and snow was on the ground. She went to her room to take off her things, but she stood instead at the window, too intent on what she had heard to be capable of anything. Her heart was almost bursting to think that Henrietta should have treasured all these years the little love she had given her, crumbs, which she had as it were left over from her husband and boys, love not even for Henrietta's own sake, but for the sake of the dead children. She with all the riches of love poured on her, and Henrietta with so little. "I was cold, selfish, self-absorbed, I didn't think of her, I forgot her, I criticized her; it was all my fault."

But even at this moment of exaltation Evelyn realized that it was not her fault, but Henrietta's own; that it was because she was so unlovable that she was so little loved.

"But if she had had the chance she wouldn't have been unlovable. She was capable of greater love than any of us, and she never had the chance. If there is any justice and mercy in the world how can they allow a poor, weak human creature to have so few opportunities, such hard temptations, and when it yields to temptation to suffer so cruelly? And now I am to go back, and be happy with Herbert and the boys, and to feel quite truly that I did everything I could, *I can't bear it.*"

She was so much filled with her thoughts that she had not observed the flight of time. She looked up, and was suddenly aware that the night had come, and that the sky was shining with innumerable stars. At the same moment she felt inextricably mingled with the stars, a rush of the most exquisite sensation, emotion, replenishment she had ever known. She felt through every fibre of her being that it was all perfectly well with Henrietta, and that the bitterness, aimlessness, and emptiness of her life was made up to her. This conviction was a thousand times more real to her than the room in which she was standing, more real than the stars, more real than herself. Tears of delight came raining down her cheeks, and she found that she was saying over and over again, "Darling, I am so glad"; poor childish words, but no more inadequate than the noblest in the language to express her unspeakable comfort, beyond all utterance, even beyond thought. How often she said these words, or how long this bliss lasted she could not tell.

A strange dream-like remembrance of it

stayed with her for some days. She told her husband, and he said, " I am very glad of anything that can be a comfort to you, dearest;" but he looked at her anxiously, and thought it was a sign that she was to be ill again. However, she continued well and strong. She told no one else, but from henceforth she was perfectly happy about Henrietta.